REHEARSALS FOR RETRIBUTION

A CAPE COD CRIME MYSTERY

Rehearsals for Retribution
A Cape Cod Crime Mystery

By
Christine Webb-Curtis
and
Dimity Hammon

Copyright 2013

Dedications

To my great aunt Addie Mae Brown, high school Latin and English teacher and the person who sparked in me a love of the written and spoken word-- long gone but never forgotten; and Theodore A. Webb, my father--minister, author and wordsmith.

To Sam and Sophie who witnessed the book's beginning; and Jack Hammon, my father—minister, author and wordsmith.

Rehearsals for Retribution

Introduction

The veteran actor gunned his Jaguar as he exited the Bourne Bridge and headed down the narrow winding road to Falmouth. He was thoroughly enjoying the way the classic English roadster clung to the road at speeds that would put an ordinary car in the ditch. He mused about his decision to come to the Cape. The North Shore was more to his liking. The Cape was hot and crowded with lots of children and their protective parents hoping to bump into someone famous. But he needed the work; and while summer stock didn't pay as much as Broadway or film, the Falmouth Playhouse always got a lot of press in the right places and it was an enjoyable break from the rigors of Hollywood. The idea was to get himself out there in the hopes he would be contacted for a more lucrative role in the fall.

The actress was beautiful, talented and hungry for revenge. For years, she had been waiting for a chance to make her nemesis pay. Now her chance had arrived. The question was how and when. She preferred her life on the west coast to time spent on Cape Cod. She was here for a purpose, however, and she hadn't planned to lose sight of that purpose. Fate had a way of dealing the deck efficiently, she believed. And she planned to take full advantage of it.

Christine Webb-Curtis and Dimity Hammon

murderer whoever we want, whenever we want."

"Oh," she said. "What fun!"

¤ ¤ ¤

Rhys Traynor was happy to take on this gig. Despite all appearances to the contrary, he needed money as usual. Born in a small, remote village in Wales, as a small boy he was charming, handsome and precocious. All those attributes followed him into adulthood. He suffered an injury to his foot as a child and walked with a cane, which he used to his advantage throughout his life.

Rhys was a brilliant student, ultimately attending Oxford and eventually receiving a scholarship to attend Harvard where he pursued an advanced degree. After leaving Harvard with a doctorate in philosophy, he did a short stint as a professor at Hunter College but found that he didn't have a penchant for the tedium of teaching. While there, he appeared in one of the school's productions and was surprisingly good. A casting agent, who happened to be in the audience to see his daughter perform, approached Rhys about pursuing an acting career. His charm and edgy sophistication made him very attractive to directors and producers, affording him many parts on stage and screen. Well suited for both, he presented quite a marketable package. He had a exceptional command of the English language, a unique and handsome appearance with a shock of prematurely white hair, and he was able to use the cane to enhance his appeal. As a bonus acting provided him access to ingénues who were young and naïve and flattered by his attention--at first. All told, he enjoyed a successful bicoastal professional career.

□ □ □

Rhys had been married to Annie's Aunt Gwen. After her death at 27, he remained Annie's father's only connection with his sister. Especially since the loss of Annie's brother to leukemia a few years previously, her parents were desperate to hang on to any shred of family.

Annie's father had another sister—younger than Gwen, who left home as soon as she was old enough. Despite all of his efforts to find her, she had apparently disappeared from the face of the earth. Shortly before his death, he had expressed his wish to Annie that she keep looking for her aunt if anything ever happened to him. Annie promised she would, but so far had had no luck. It was a constant source of sadness for her. Somehow she was sure if she ever found her aunt, she would be as loving and generous as her father.

Rhys remarried soon after his first wife's death. Gwen had moved to Hollywood with Rhys and allegedly died of a drug overdose—something that seemed very out of character to those who knew her. However, for the L.A. coroner, death by drugs was commonplace, and there had been no cause for further investigation. His second wife disappeared suddenly while at Rhys' summer place in Ipswich, Massachusetts, never to be heard from again. Rhys had been heartbroken and vowed never to remarry. But he continued to enjoy the company of women and spent time with a series of young, blond, beautiful starlets who hoped he could make them famous.

Christine Webb-Curtis and Dimity Hammon

Chapter 2 -- The Detective Gets a Gig

Joe thought that his friend, Detective Nico Forgione, would be perfect in the role of Colonel Mustard in the play. He waited to call Nico with his proposal until he knew he would be home and relaxing with a pre-dinner cocktail.

Nico had arrived on the Cape the previous summer per doctor's order to spend a few weeks vacationing with his wife, Lil, at Lawson's Golf Resort. What he thought was going to be enforced relaxation for a few weeks turned into an unexpected investigation into the death of a porn star from California who was on the Cape with her movie director boyfriend, Joe Putnam. The Falmouth Police Department's only detective was in Italy at his daughter's wedding, so Police Chief Adam Mercer called in his chits with the Boston Police Department Chief to see if Nico could help on the investigation. Since Nico wasn't much of a vacationer and the trip hadn't actually been his choice, he welcomed the opportunity.

Midway into the investigation, Falmouth's detective, Sean Spencer, decided to throw in the towel and stay in Italy with his Italian-born wife and only child so he could be around to enjoy his future grandchildren. Nico was subsequently offered Spencer's job on very good terms. He was able to simply transfer his benefit package from Boston to Falmouth without interruption, and he was allowed whatever time he needed to make a decision on whether or not he might be willing to accept the position permanently.

To sweeten the pot, Spencer offered to make his house available on a long-term lease to Nico. He didn't plan to come back to the Cape, but he wanted to leave open the option that his daughter and son-in-law might someday return. And considering that the house was originally built by his ship's captain great grandfather, he naturally wanted to retain his family's legacy as long as there was family to inherit and enjoy it.

¤ ¤ ¤

It was lovely outside so Nico and Lil decided to take their evening cocktails up on the widow's walk that graced the roof like the top tier of a wedding cake. They grabbed the phone for the inevitable call that otherwise would have had them racing down the precarious spiral staircase. The widow's walk had been well used early in the home's life and while the Spencers rarely made the climb to the top, the Forgiones found it to be magical. It gave them a new appreciation and affection for the savage sea.

The house had been built in 1864 when Abraham Lincoln was president and shipping was the lifeline for any luxuries in the lives of Americans who paid dearly for the privilege. Spencer's great grandfather was a successful shipping entrepreneur based in Boston. He and his family lived on Cape Cod—a short run by boat from Boston. He had built a house that reflected his success and the space needs for his growing family. It was located on the bay facing Martha's Vineyard. Far enough from the shore to avoid the ravages of inclement weather, it was close enough to allow an unobstructed view and private access to the sea.

On the way to the roof, they passed the three third-floor bedrooms previously kept for hired help—housekeeper, cook and nanny in the early years and housekeeper and cook for the next generation. Lil smiled at Nico as they passed the rooms. "I can't wait to have the grandbabies here this summer. They love having this whole floor to themselves."

There was a narrow back staircase leading down to the kitchen that had been used mainly by the staff in the past, but was now purely for the amusement of the little ones. On the second floor, there were five bedrooms built around a central staircase plus a sunroom and a small library.

It was a glorious house, and Nico and Lil enjoyed every amenity and comfort. They felt it was the perfect place to wind down a successful, if stressful, career as long as Sean Spencer would allow. Just as they sat down in their deck chairs, the cordless phone rang.

"I hope that's not a work call, Nico," said Lil.

"Or one of your church friends calling to plan for yet another scheme to save the world," replied Nico.

¤ ¤ ¤

Nico and Lil had settled into their new community over the past year. Lil found a spiritual home at St. Mark's Catholic Church. She virtually took over the Social Justice Committee and was establishing herself as quite the mover and shaker in the Cape Cod Catholic community. In addition, she was chair of the Dorothy Day Service Center, collaborating with local food banks to ensure that the poor of Falmouth and the Cape were able to keep food on their tables. She was making a mark in her new home.

While Nico was not to see such a well-publicized investigation throughout the winter as he had experienced the previous summer, he had a good eleven or so months to settle into the job. He had come to enjoy his colleague and subordinate, Patrick

Kellerman, and often invited him and his partner, Marc Brand, for Sunday dinner with his family. They fit in quite nicely with the Forgione clan. These were regular mixed-culture affairs—the Italians and the Irishman--and Marc, the mongrel, mixed-background bloke. Nico was able to get to know the local resources and geography, connect with the other police departments on the Cape, and prepare himself for whatever might come next. His Altoids habit had moved to the background of his days along with the less stressful regimen of crime on Cape Cod.

Their children visited them on the Cape almost as much as they had in Boston. Their oldest daughter and her husband and children still showed up most Sundays for a late lunch and an afternoon visit. Their son and his wife and children came usually every other Sunday at the same time. And their other daughter visited about once a month—usually coming on Saturday morning and staying through Sunday night despite having to deal with the hellish commute back to Boston on Monday morning. Nico continued to cook his Sunday meal with pleasure. And it was received with equal pleasure by family and friends.

All in all, Nico and Lil had become real Cape residents and found it very much to their liking. They were well-suited to the sea, the sand, the easier pace, and the hospitality of Cape citizenry. They had no regrets about their sudden departure from Boston and Nico's job. It was the right thing at the right time.

Joe and Nico had become friends after the fiasco with the investigation into the death of Joe's then girlfriend, Celine. Speculation was that she had been murdered, and Joe was the prime suspect. It proved to be a difficult and confusing case that involved the usual motivations--drugs, jealousy and love gone wrong; but Nico's detective skills finally led to the unlikely murderer. His investigation proved Joe's innocence, and as friends, they bonded over their love of cooking and fine wine.

Joe needed one more cast member and figured it was worth a shot to give Nico a call and ask him if he would be interested in becoming an actor in the play *Clue*—especially since he had a penchant for the theatre—albeit from the perspective of the plush seats out front.

When the phone rang right after they sat down with their drinks to enjoy the view from the widow's walk, Nico looked at the caller ID and answered, "Hey, Joe. How's the production coming? I'm looking forward to it."

"I'm actually calling about the production. We're doing *Clue*, by the way."

"Oh?"

"There's a role in the play that I've had a little trouble filling, and I thought that since you're such a fan of the theatre, you might be interested in stepping in."

"Me? I don't know, Joe. It's been a long time since my one high school acting experience. It certainly wasn't noteworthy. I'm flattered, though."

"I'd like to think that part of being a good director is finding people who can act— not necessarily people who have always been acting. And I figure you do a lot of that already in your detective work."

"What exactly do you mean, Joe? Are you saying I'm not sincere in my work?"

"No. But I suggest that when you're interviewing someone as part of an investigation, you have a certain way of putting them at ease. Part of that is pretending you are interested in or concerned about what they're interested in or concerned about. Right?"

"Point well taken, I suppose. But I do have a job, y'know. It isn't as if I can just take off."

"Come on, Nico. Exactly how hot is the crime scene at the moment? I haven't noticed any police cars careening around Falmouth recently."

"Another point, I suppose. But if I agreed, my work would always have to come first."

"I'm willing to take that risk. And thanks."

"So what's first, then? Do I have to report somewhere? Can you get me a script? Are you already in rehearsals? Or do I have a little time?"

"I'll get you a script later today. We're starting rehearsals tomorrow—just a very easy run-through."

"I can't memorize anything by tomorrow! Geez, Joe, maybe this isn't such a good idea."

"No. It's fine. We'll rehearse with our scripts for a while before we go cold turkey. You'll have plenty of time to get up to speed. Really."

"If you say so, then. Bring me the script later this evening and I'll give it a shot."

"I really am indebted to you—again!"

"Right. Well, I expect at least a dinner out of this—that is, prepared by you. None of this taking me out to the pizza joint."

"OK. You drive a hard bargain, but you're on. I'll see you this evening."

¤ ¤ ¤

When they finished their drinks, they headed back downstairs anticipating dinner. Lil stopped in their bedroom for a sweater and found Nico in the kitchen, a welcoming and well-used space by both the previous and current residents.

"So, what have you dreamed up for dinner?" asked Lil. She looked around the kitchen for clues. The kitchen was glass-enclosed on the exterior walls—a remodel in the first few years of the 21st century--and shared the same view as the living room-- directly out to the sea. Both the kitchen and the butler's pantry sported the original slate counters and sinks with the addition of a garbage disposal and stylish and updated faucets. The floors throughout the entire house were wide pine boards well-worn and buffed to a lovely soft sheen. Nico looked up from the chopping block and winked.

"Have I ever let you down, Cara? I'm not too sure of my acting skills, but I hardly ever worry about my cooking skills!"

The appliances were all updated and glass-fronted upper cabinetry was up against the inside walls in order not to obscure the view. Above the windows sat a plate rail where seldom-used platters and serving dishes were displayed. Outside the kitchen windows were window boxes containing brilliant red geraniums—prolific in season. The boxes were taken down in the winter for storage in the garden shed. Nico loved to cook in this open and airy space—so different from their home in Boston.

"Just curious—and hungry, of course."

"I have something special planned. How 'bout you just wait and see."

"That sounds like something worth waiting for."

Later Nico and Lil sat out on the porch to enjoy an after-dinner drink.

"Another spectacular meal, Detective. Thank you for feeding my appetite as well as my soul."

"My pleasure, Cara. As always."

Just as they raised their glasses, Joe Putnam arrived. Lil went to the door and welcomed him inside.

"Joe, we were just enjoying a limoncello. Would you care to join us?" Said Lil.

"I'd like that. I haven't had one since I was last on the Amalfi Coast."

"Wonderful. Nico is sitting on the porch. I know you came to talk to him. I'll be right out. You know the way," said Lil waving her arm in the direction of the porch.

Joe walked into the living room through the double French doors. The room was bright and open and faced the sea at the back. On the outside wall sat a large open fireplace with a cherry wood mantel and surround, which was lovingly used by all generations of residents in both winter and summer to ward off the cold breezes and storms coming off Vineyard Bay. Two bay windows adorned the front and back walls, and window seats provided children with a comfortable place to read their books and storage below for the board games that everyone played on a stormy evening.

Through the French doors to the outside, Joe stepped onto the open porch, which was used on warm days on a regular basis. The porch had a hanging bench swing that had been replaced several times and was held in high regard by all who used it. The swing faced out to the sea and was a favorite place for reading, talking, courting and the like.

Stepping out to the porch, Joe said, "Evening, Nico. Lil said you were out here."

"Joe. Come on out," Nico said getting to his feet and offering his hand.

"Sit down, Nico," said Joe grasping his hand. "Here's the script for you. I thought you'd like to talk about it a little first."

"Well, yes I would. I was telling Lil this evening about it and realized I didn't even know the part you'd asked me to play."

"Sorry about that. I wasn't specific on the phone, but I'd like to have you take on the role of Colonel Mustard. It wasn't until the end of the day when I finally cast the other parts that I realized this is the part for you."

"And why is that?"

"You bring a certain military presence to the stage, I think. And you're about the right look for the part as well. I think it suits you."

"OK. Well, then, I know what to work on. But can you tell me a little about the character. I haven't seen the play in years."

Lil arrived with the limoncello. Joe stood up and thanked her.

"Mind if I join you, gentlemen?"

"Not at all," said Joe.

"Have you finished casting the play, Joe?" asked Lil.

"All but one role, and the two most minor characters. Did you want to know who's in it?"

"As a matter of fact, I like to keep up on these things," said Lil with a playful wink.

"Sure you do, Lil. Don't tell me you're starting a new column for the 'Falmouth Fanatic' or some such rag," he said with a sly grin. "And by the way, this is much better than any limoncello I remember having in Italy."

"Thanks. It's Nico's special concoction. I agree that it's the best."

"Well, Nico. You are quite the Renaissance man, aren't you?"

"I try. . ."

"Back to the play, then. The people whose names you know from the acting world are Rhys Traynor, who's playing the role of Professor Plum."

"Nice catch."

"And Troy Douglas who's playing the butler."

"Charming, I suppose," said Lil.

"And Dolores Darrington will be playing Miss Scarlet. She ought to be quite good—as long as there are no mishaps."

"Why d'you say that, Joe?" asked Nico.

"She has something of a reputation, Caro, for injuring herself—or others—on a stage or movie set," explained Lil. "It makes for an interesting production, I'll bet. Eh, Joe."

"Indeed it does. We always have to prepare for contingencies with Dolores. However, she is a very talented actor."

"One more actor is Eric Shiller. You know him, of course, Nico. He's the actor who worked with Celine and followed us here last summer."

"Yes. Seemed like a nice guy."

"Yeah. He's a real innocent despite his run in X-rated films. I cast him in a movie I filmed last winter. He did a nice job. He really only needed a break and sure can use the money. And his family is joining him here, too."

"That's great. Did you tell me that his daughter was ill, Nico?" asked Lil.

Joe responded for Nico. "She's much improved. And they have a baby son now as well. All healthy."

"Good for them, then," said Lil. "They deserve some happiness."

"Yes, they do," agreed Joe. "So, then for local people, I have Bertha Poppe playing Yvette, the maid."

"That's courageous of you, Joe," Lil interjected.

"So I found out—but after I'd already cast her. Ted Dickenson is taking on the role of Mr. Boddy."

"Oh good for you, Joe. Does his dog have a part, too?"

Joe chuckled. "No, Casey'll have to sit this one out, though I'm sure he could barge in unannounced at any point in the play."

They shared his chuckle. Casey, as the local wandering pooch, seemed to find his way into all sorts of trouble as they had found out the previous summer.

"Then who else is left? Susan Dickenson is going to be our Miss Peacock. And for the other small roles, I'll get someone else local."

Christine Webb-Curtis and Dimity Hammon

Chapter 3 -- Beginnings

After their marriage Annie Cushman moved out of her little house in East Falmouth and into Joe's home on Vineyard Sound for the summer. Joe had grown up in Boston and Cape Cod. Once his films had taken off, he worked most of the time in Los Angeles. But during the summer, Joe always returned to Cape Cod, in part to produce the summer plays at the Falmouth Playhouse. Now that he and Annie were married, they were seasonally bicoastal. Annie kept ownership of her restaurant/tourist shop in town, the Fair Falmouth Café; but with their new baby, she turned over the day-to-day operations to a trusted employee and a couple of good summer students.

Sophie Cushman Putnam was born in April, four months after Joe and Annie's wedding. It was a New Year's Day wedding and took place at their Cape Cod home overlooking the water. It seemed that most of Falmouth was invited. Joe's house was plenty big enough to accommodate the affair, but an insulated tent had been put up on the lawn with a covered passageway into the house. After the ceremony, the guests retired to the tent for dinner and dancing. It was one of those affairs that was simply joyous. There were no flaws, no bad feelings, no awkward moments, no regrets. Joe and Annie's family had become whole again.

Annie and Joe spent the spring in California where Sophie was born in what the doctors had called, because of Annie's advanced age, a "risky" pregnancy and delivery but which was, in fact, problem free. In Falmouth, Joe arranged for the rental of a space in town near the café where Annie could establish her own studio to work on her sculpture once again without interruption. She hadn't spent too much time there yet as Sophie was still nursing, and anyway, she was enjoying the luxury of being with her baby without the pressure of working.

Annie's house was rented to her son Josiah's best friend, Sam Wilson, with the understanding that Josiah would live there when he was home from school for the summer. Sam had worked at Lawson's Inn and Golf Resort for several years but continued to live at home with his parents. He was more than grateful for the ridiculously low rent and the privacy he was afforded at Annie's house. Living with his parents had not been his cup of tea, and he was thrilled to be on his own to pursue his own interests without the interference of his brothers and parents. He recently developed a fascination for fine cabinet making and was hoping to apprentice with Naoki Tashima, a local and sought-after craftsman who was too arthritic to do much work himself. Tashima's son did not aspire to pick up the awl and saw as his father had and instead was a well-respected Cape architect.

Sam met both Tashimas at Joe and Annie's wedding and expressed great admiration for the elder Tashima's craft. He told Mr. Tashima of his long-standing interest in fine cabinetry making and that he would work for him for free as long as he was able to continue his regular job. Mr. Tashima agreed and also said that if he excelled, he might eventually take him on as a paid apprentice. It appeared that Sam had found his calling. Over the last several months, he purchased tools to practice at home whenever he had the time. He was beginning to actually do some very basic work that Mr. Tashima found promising.

Because Joe and Annie were in California after their wedding, Josiah spent his spring break there instead of Cape Cod. He wanted to get to know Los Angeles and its environs and become acquainted with his miraculous new sister. Josiah returned to the Cape for the summer as soon as the semester ended and he and Sam were settling back into their routine. Josiah even agreed to teach Sam how to cook. Sam was turning into a regular sophisticate.

◻ ◻ ◻

Rhys' home was located off Beacon Street in Brookline on a lovely tree-lined street with other large well-maintained homes. The gracious brick house was built in the 1920s, and was a wonderful combination of the craftsman-style use of wood and natural materials and the concept that rooms should be separate, but large and welcoming. Because he could no longer afford his home, he had it on the market for well over a million dollars. Its proximity to both Boston University and Boston College meant plenty of interesting venues for fun and socializing. On warm summer nights, Rhys could sit on his patio and hear the Red Sox game at Fenway Park.

Rhys had been out with his old friend Buddy Fazio that evening and had overindulged at the bar. Returning home very carefully and definitely over the blood alcohol limit, he pulled into the alley behind the house and slowly made his way to the two-car garage—a luxury in town. He pulled in at an awkward angle and, almost rolled out of the car. He entered the house through the well-used laundry room into the massive kitchen complete with a wide island, several ovens and a kitchen nook. Rummaging through the pantry for a bag of crisps, he wended his way through the spacious butler's pantry where the china was stored, picking up yet another Guinness along the way. Weaving through the welcoming dining room that boasted a large bay window with French doors opening onto a small front patio, he stumbled into the library where he collapsed in his well-worn club chair in front of the magnificent fireplace and surrounded by floor-to-ceiling oak bookcases along all the walls. It was the place where guests would gather for cocktails and evening entertainment.

Sated but still drunk, he staggered into the entrance hall, which boasted the original Egyptian-themed hand-painted wallpaper, and pulled himself up the lovely but--in his condition--challenging curving staircase. Upstairs were four large bedrooms, each with its own tiled bath. Bracing himself along the wall, he made his way to the largest bedroom where he collapsed on the bed.

While Rhys loved the Brookline house, he escaped as often as possible to his cottage on Great Neck in Ipswich. Though he couldn't really afford either house, his cottage was disarmingly simple compared to the Brookline house. Also for sale, it had a kitchen, combination living room/dining room, two bedrooms, one of which had originally been the garage, and a small bathroom that required guests to take numbers. The screened-in porch was where most people gathered, and there was rarely a time when the place wasn't filled with company. Strewn around the cottage were day beds with lots of pillows where family and visitors inevitably ended up for a post-prandial nap after a lunch or dinner of the local little neck clams they had harvested in the flats in front of the cottage. Often the clams were accompanied by haddock or flounder caught in the bay on the way back from boat trips to nearby Crane's Beach and Castle or Plum Island. The rule was that if you took the boat out, you had to bring something home for dinner.

The train from Boston could get to Ipswich in an hour, and the five o'clock Pullman served up perfect martinis. Shuttle duty to the train station rotated among guests until everyone arrived. All summer the cottage was filled with smart, sophisticated guests from all walks of life who enjoyed the spectacular setting and fun atmosphere of Rhys' getaway.

Each of Rhys' homes was graced by his current ravishing lady love. Although never lasting more than a few months, the lucky ones came on the scene in the late spring so they could spend time at both the cottage and the Brookline house. There was no paid staff in Ipswich, and the current beauty was expected to be responsible for kitchen duty. Rhys never warned them about those chores and the results were sometimes laughable and often inedible. Fortunately, there were several good restaurants in Ipswich.

Christine Webb-Curtis and Dimity Hammon

Chapter 4 -- Dixie Comes and Goes

Madison Dunham and Brittany Scott arrived late in the afternoon and were settling in. This was their second year working for the summer at Lawson's. The previous summer, the girls had become chummy with Josiah Cushman and Sam Wilson who both worked at Lawson's golf course. Sam was the full-time greens keeper and Josiah did whatever odd job was needed from retrieving balls from the driving range, to refilling the ball machine, to collecting carts that had been left here and there by hotel guests. Josiah had just finished his sophomore year at Bowdoin, so he and Madison had easily fallen in together in anticipation of her first and his third year of college. They were not exclusive but saw a lot of each other even so. By default, Sam and Brittany had gone out a couple of times the summer before; but they hadn't gotten to know each other well. Brittany hoped to remedy that this summer.

The four of them were thrown together the year before when they discovered a dead body on the beach—Joe Putnam's then girlfriend from California. It had shaken the normally quiet resort town, and the girls demonstrated their skill at observation when helping to solve the crime. In their opinion they solved it single-handedly.

During their first year at Lawson's, the girls earned their stripes as chambermaids, and this year, they graduated to waitresses, or serving staff as they were called. They were hoping to get some evening shifts right away since the tips were much higher, but they were being tested on the morning and lunch shifts before being allowed access to the higher-priced fare. Instead of staying in the dorm that was located adjacent to the Inn as they had the summer before, they rented a little cottage on Onion Bay in East Falmouth for the summer. It was on a shallow bay that virtually emptied out at low tide and then, it seemed, when their backs were turned, refilled to obliterate the view from only a few hours before. The cottage was a cozy one-story structure with two bedrooms at the back of the house, a utilitarian kitchen and an eating area in the front. A small living room filled the other quarter of the cottage and had a fireplace which faced the bay. There was a little porch on the front with enough room for the predictable battered rockers and hammock hooks.

There were no cottages to the east of their place and to the west there was an identical cottage that appeared to be uninhabited. The grass was overgrown all around, and there were no flowerpots or any other sign of life. Its only distinctive feature was an attached garage.

The girls had brought their necessary treasures to complement the furnishings of the cottage, including duvets, iPod speakers, pillows, throws and most unexpectedly and much to Madison's surprise, Brittany's cat, Dixie.

Dixie was a petite, pretty tabby that Brittany rescued from certain death at the local SPCA in Lewiston, Maine, where she was a student at Bates College. She assumed that her parents would take care of the cat during the summer, but they had just rescued a Mini-Schnauzer with a hatred for cats. Left in the lurch, Brittany tried to convince Madison's parents to take Dixie for the summer, but they were in new love with their darling Bichon Frise and had no interest in spreading their affection to a temporary cat. The owners of the cottage had a "no pet" rule but lived in New York and were unlikely to visit without notice. Brittany figured she could put the cat somewhere out of the way if they came to check. Dixie spent her kittyhood outdoors and believed it was her right to come and go as she pleased. The girls presumed she would know her way around after a few days and could help out by keeping the mouse population down. As a safety precaution in the meantime, they locked her and her litter box in Brittany's room.

The cottage was well-equipped with an older but serviceable fridge and a decent stove in the kitchen. There was even a microwave-- a necessity for the girls who cooked little and were unlikely to learn over the summer. Each bedroom had a twin bed, bureau and small closet. The living room had the requisite old saggy sofa, two equally saggy chairs and a desk. There was a worn braid rug on the hardwood floor and a couple of old mismatched lamps that were plenty good enough for reading. A bookshelf sat in the corner filled with summer reading left by other occupants from previous years. All in all it was perfect for Brittany and Madison.

Both girls managed to get decent grades during their freshman year—Brittany at Bates and Madison at Bowdoin College. Nonetheless, they paid considerable attention to freshman partying, and the consequences could have been much more grave. Fortunately they advanced to their sophomore years in good standing with the colleges and, more importantly, their parents.

They were looking forward to ushering at the Falmouth Playhouse again this summer as was the custom and privilege for Lawson's summer workers.

¤ ¤ ¤

Later than they intended and after one more beer on the porch, the girls stumbled into the cottage exhausted.

"Geez, Maddy. It's so stuffy. I don't think this place was opened up all winter. We've gotta get some air in here."

"I totally agree. Maybe we could open that high window over the refrigerator."

"Good idea, Maddy." Brittany looked up. "But it doesn't have a screen. What if Dixie gets out?"

"I don't think the kitty would even notice it. I'll grab a chair and get it open."

"Well, o.k. I'll sneak into my room just in case and keep the door closed."

Brittany carefully cracked the door to her room. Like any self-respecting feline, Dixie shot out through the door, disappearing into the kitchen.

"Damn. Maddy. Help. She got right past me!"

Madison hurried back out of her room just in time to see the cat squeeze through the open window to freedom. Seeing there was nothing she could do, she said, "It's too late and too dark to chase her around, Brit. She'll find her way and come back in the morning when she's hungry."

"I suppose," Brittany said glumly. "G'night."

"G'night, Brit. It'll be all right."

¤ ¤ ¤

Dixie was delighted to find her way outside. She peered around to get her bearings. 'Sometimes these humans are really stupid,' she thought, as if she couldn't find her way back to where the food and her bed was. 'Really!!'

She prowled around the potential hunting grounds as well as hiding places--just in case. She could see lots of good places to find little critters, although the area was a bit short of trees to climb if and when escape became necessary.

Just as she spotted a garter snake slithering along in the grassy center of the road, trouble meandered around the bend in the lane in the form of a large dog. Casey, the golden retriever, had gotten himself into a bit of trouble the previous summer while running around unsupervised. While his owners, Ted and Susan Dickenson, thought they had done as much as humanly possible since then to keep him under control, Casey more than once evaded all their best efforts at imprisonment and roamed the neighborhood at will. Everyone loved Casey with the exception of the lady down the road from the

Dickensons. She had a garden of prized Dahlias for which Casey had no appreciation as he joyfully galloped through without a care, leaving disaster in his wake.

On this particular night Casey was bored. He deftly opened his kennel door and trooped out to scope out his territory and beyond. Easily distracted, he got a whiff of one of his favorite playthings--cat. Dixie sensed danger and took off back toward the girls' cottage, but Casey spotted her and took up the chase. Just as Casey was closing in on her puffy tail, she took a last-minute diversionary turn and scooted in through a tiny opening at the bottom of the neighbor's garage door. She squeezed through with difficulty, forcing her to reevaluate her departure through the same opening. Casey snuffled at the opening for a while but quickly gave up the chase and moved on in search of other adventures. Dixie was relieved that she had escaped the dog, though she never would have expected any other outcome. Dogs were just plain dumb and she knew she would have no problem in the future. She considered dogs to be sport--no real threat.

¤ ¤ ¤

Brittany woke up the next morning to find that the cat had not returned. Knowing that Dixie loved her creature comforts--like food and a soft bed, Brittany assumed she

would have come back by morning. Madison
stumbled out of her room. She hadn't seen
Dixie either. The girls had to be at work by
six--an ungodly hour to college coeds, so by
the time they had showered, put on their
makeup and dressed in a rush, Dixie was no
longer a priority.

Their boss, April Butler, or Ms. Butler
to them, was impressed that the girls had
reported for duty on time. Though this habit
would not likely continue through the
summer, ignorance was temporarily bliss for
Ms. Butler. She instructed them in the
breakfast service drill and then went on about
her business while keeping an eagle eye on
their progress. Lawson's was open year-
round, but since golf was the big draw,
summer was the busy season. The Inn was
only half full this early, which gave Madison
and Brittany plenty of time to perfect their
waitressing skills. By the end of the morning,
they were ready to try the one-handed tray
whoosh they always saw on TV. The result
was jarringly noisy—especially for the early
morning diners, and they spent the next half
hour cleaning up the mess and apologizing to
their glaring boss, other staff, and their
customers.

In spite of their little accident, the girls
were able to take a break between breakfast
and lunch and used the time to drive down to

the beach near the Putnam house where they had often gone the previous summer. They parked and headed down to the beach for a quick chance to get their feet wet. Hearing a shout, they turned to see Josiah and Sam coming up the beach. The boys were working late that day and had taken advantage of the time to take in a swim before they had to show up at Lawson's.

"Hey Brit, Maddy, great to see you! When d'you get here?" Josiah said as he gave Madison a quick hug and somewhat self-conscious kiss.

"Hi Jos, hi Sam," replied Madison. "We got in last night and had to be at the Inn at six this morning--if you can believe that!"

"Welcome to the world of high-paid waitresses, ladies," Sam chirped, happy to have the girls there for the summer.

"Really," said Brittany. "And speaking of that, we need to get back to work, Maddy, or we'll get fired, especially after our little spill this morning!"

The boys knew better than to ask questions about any spill.

"Hey guys, why don't you come down to our place tonight for a few beers? Maddy told you where we are, didn't she?"

"Yeah. I heard when we were at school," said Josiah.

"OK, then. Does that work for you?"

"Great," the boys said in unison and headed back to their towels.

The girls hurried back to their car delighted that they had moved so easily back into the pace of the summer and its social life with Sam and Josiah.

¤ ¤ ¤

At the end of their afternoon shift, Brittany was eager to get home and find Dixie. She was worried sick that her cat was in trouble someplace and hoped that she would find her sitting on the porch flicking her tail when they got home. No such luck though. Dixie was nowhere to be found.

Despite their exhaustion the girls set out immediately to find her. They walked down the beach thinking that she might have been stalking some little bird and gotten caught in the mud somehow at the top of the bay, but she wasn't there. They split up and searched the dunes and into the wooded area behind the cottage. Still no luck.

"D'ya think she could have gotten inside someone's house," asked Madison?

"I can't imagine how, but who knows? Let's take a look around the cottage next door."

"OK, but let's hurry. That place gives me the creeps."

The girls went around to the front porch of the cottage, checking carefully that there was no one home. They cautiously peeked under the decrepit hot tub cover certain they would find her there--drowned.

They breathed a sigh of relief when she wasn't there and continued around to the far side peering behind the bushes and junk that had accumulated. Then they walked around the attached garage calling to the cat all the time.

"Oh no," wailed Brittany. "Do you think she's disappeared forever? I feel so bad. I never should have brought her. It'll be all my fault if something happens to her!"

"Take it easy. She's around here somewhere. We just need to keep looking," soothed Madison.

As they rounded the other side of the house, they heard a faint mewing sound. The girls called louder and then saw her sitting on the sill of a small window high up on the side of the garage.

"Oh, thank god. There she is. Bad kitty! You must be starving!"

Dixie mewed loudly and scratched at the window in reply.

"Now what?" cried Brittany, "How will we ever get her out? Poor baby. We have to get her. What're we gonna do?"

For once Madison was stymied. The house was locked up tight. The window was too high for them to reach; and, in any case it didn't look as if it would open.

"Maybe if we had a ladder, we could break the window?"

"Yeah. But let's leave that as a last resort. Where would we get a ladder anyway?"

"Maybe the guys could help us out. There's gotta be a ladder at Sam's place."

"Sure, but they're both working and won't be finished until much later this afternoon. I don't think they'd appreciate us calling them to leave work for your cat!"

"I guess you're right, but we have to do something. We can't just leave her. She's crying!"

"Lookit, Brit, we can't do anything right now, and it's gotta be making it worse standing here where she can see us. Let's go home and think about it. We'll figure out something."

Brittany agreed reluctantly and they trudged back to their cottage.

Rehearsals for Retribution

In the meantime out on Vineyard Bay, four guys in a speedboat full of drugs were racing to get to the deserted house on Onion Bay before the tide went out.

Christine Webb-Curtis and Dimity Hammon

Chapter 5 – Casting

Joe decided that instead of hiring actors to suit the roles in Clue, he would adapt the roles to suit his actors. That seemed particularly appropriate after Troy Douglas' agent, Lenny Levine, called.

Troy Douglas wanted the part of the butler in the worst way. An over-the-top gay actor, he was sought by casting directors who were looking for a stereotypical gay character. He had no shortage of work and was very popular in the entertainment media. His charitable causes were AIDS prevention and protection of abused animals. He was able to attract big money for both and was willing to put in the time and effort necessary to help in those efforts, attending dinners, signing autographs, and personally soliciting donations from influential and wealthy patrons. His designer-clad Yorkie brought a certain panache to his appearances.

He began his acting in high school in an effort to ward off the ridicule he experienced and realized that he made an impact with his exaggerated characterizations. As a result, after years of repressed homosexuality, he came into his own as a swishy and colorful queen teen. He didn't receive widespread acceptance but developed a small bevy of artistic girls who saw him as a non-threatening male peer confidant. In his senior year, he was the lead in a wildly popular production of "La Cage aux Folles." The brother-in-law of a member of the audience was a casting director in New York, and the rest is history.

Along the way, Troy had become dissatisfied with his acting career and nearly gave it all up until he stumbled across a performance by Rhys Traynor. Traynor had portrayed a man conflicted about his sexuality, struggling with his ultimate decision to remain in a heterosexual relationship despite all indications of his unresolved homosexual desires. Douglas was taken in by the portrayal and felt sure that it described Traynor's real sexual tendencies. He was very attracted to this oh-so-handsome actor and had since looked for opportunities to guide him toward his true sexual persona.

When Douglas heard that Traynor was in one of Joe Putnam's productions at the Falmouth Playhouse, he called his agent. "Lenny!" shrieked Troy. "I've got to be cast in Putnam's summer production of *Clue*."

"Troy, calm down! Get a grip."

"Look. Rhys Traynor is in that production and I insist that you get me a place in the cast."

"I'll see what I can do, Troy. I'm sure I can find something."

"Oh, no. Not something. It's gotta be the butler. I've gotta be the butler. That's the only part I want. I'll even take a reduced rate if I can have the part of the butler."

"What's the appeal of the butler, then?"

"Never mind. That's the part I want and the only one I want. Make it happen, Lenny!"

"OK. I'll see what I can do."

"Well, dear, if you value me as a client, you'll get it done. I'm not fooling around here. It's gotta be a go. Not interested in Mr. Green. Not interested in Professor Plum. It's Wadsworth or nothing. Got it?"

"OK. I said I'd call."

"I'm just trying to make you understand. I'm not interested in any of the other parts."

Lenny sighed and did as requested knowing he would never hear the end of it if he didn't. To his surprise Putnam agreed that Troy would be the perfect butler. Naturally Lenny didn't mention Troy's inexplicable enthusiasm for the role.

Joe realized then that this production of *Clue* might be a bit different.

¤ ¤ ¤

Dolores Darrington made it obvious through the Hollywood grapevine that she was planning to spend the summer on Cape Cod and she hoped she wouldn't be too bored. Joe contacted her agent—the same Lenny Levine, and was told she might be available for at least one play. Joe didn't have a huge budget for his productions and was sure he would be turned down flat when he told Lenny how much he could offer Dolores. To his great surprise--and for that matter, to Lenny's surprise--Dolores agreed quickly and signed the contract. Joe planned to cast her as Miss Scarlett.

Since her older sister's mysterious death, Dolores had grown into a beautiful woman, albeit with several alterations, including a name change. She had a very successful acting career with one Oscar nomination and three Tony's. Despite her success, she never stopped missing her sister. Their mother had died of cancer when the girls were quite young. Her sister was her best friend at a time in her childhood when that relationship was all important. Losing her beloved big sister had been like losing her mother all over again. The loss shaped her life in a way that resulted in both the drive to be successful at all costs and never-ending grief. She left home as soon as she finished high school and never contacted any of her

family again. She felt it would be too painful.
She secretly kept track of her brother,
however, and knew all about his family.
'Maybe one day when I bring my sister's killer
to justice, I'll have the courage to contact
them,' she thought. At the time of her sister's
death she claimed that she knew who
murdered her, and others agreed. The justice
system, however, played in his favor instead
of her sister's. It had failed her, too, and it
seemed so unfair.

Despite Dolores' artistry on stage and
screen, she had one unique flaw. She was
clumsy. Actually, she was very clumsy. One
might have called her a klutz. She herself
had admitted to it. The studios learned to
take out extra insurance in anticipation of the
mishap. It was never "if," but always "when"
and "how serious." They could only hope that
such a mishap would be trivial. Regrettably,
on many occasions, the cameramen would
have to go to extraordinary lengths to shoot
around Dottie's injury. And stage hands were
required to reposition furniture and props to
disguise a broken leg or wrist. The more
careful she was, it seemed, the more likely it
would happen.

Dolores' return to the Cape was a
reluctant but necessary homecoming. She
hadn't been on the Cape since before her
sister's death, but she had to take care of the
long-standing obligation once and for all.

She checked into Lawson's and asked for a cottage near her colleagues, Troy Douglas and Rhys Traynor, so they could get together in their off hours for rehearsals. The morning after arriving, she asked for an extra towel from the chambermaid who was cleaning next door.

"Also, I want to leave this little surprise for Rhys, you know. We're at the Falmouth Playhouse next week."

"Oh, that's sweet of you, Ms. Darrington. You know, I'll be ushering for you at the theatre this summer."

¤ ¤ ¤

Eric Shiller had been caught up in the intrigue of the prior summer involving the death of Joe Putnam's girlfriend. Prior to coming to Cape Cod last year, his pregnant wife and daughter were forced to return home to her parents in order to get some support and stability. Their house had been in foreclosure, and Eric was a broken man. He emerged unscathed from the police investigation and only wanted to salvage his family and his home. By the time summer ended, he had secured a part in Joe Putnam's next movie and returned from Cape Cod to Los Angeles. He was able to reverse the foreclosure on their house, and his family returned to home and hearth, at least for now.

Rehearsals for Retribution

He and Jennie had married right out of
high school back in small-town Illinois. Their
first child, Sara, had some serious medical
problems and was in and out of the hospital
when she was very little. She continued to
need medical attention from time to time,
which meant they always had to be near an
emergency medical facility. They had a new
baby a few months before--a boy who showed
no sign of having the congenital problems that
their precious little girl had. His daughter
was sweet and smart; and since the prior
summer, her heart was steadily getting
stronger with many fewer episodes requiring
hospital care.

His family had planned to join him at
the end of the summer; but Joe was paying
him enough money for them to stay in a
cottage at Lawson's for the whole season so
they could prepare their own meals and enjoy
the privacy and luxury that the Inn provided.
The only hitch had been the expense of
renting a car which they would need to get
around. After looking at all of the big name
companies, Eric found a great deal at Rent-A-
Wreck--an old, but serviceable red Toyota
Corolla. He was glad that he would not have
to suffer the loneliness that is the drudgery of
most actors and their families when they are
filming on location. He was so looking
forward to having them out in the audience
smiling and proud of him.

This summer, Eric planned to take full advantage of his opportunity to work again with Joe and to be the best Mr. Green ever. As always he continued to be strapped for money to cover his daughter's medical treatments. When he was approached by someone who wanted to pay him a good deal of money to use his car once in a while, he was happy to oblige. The extra money would be a big bonus without much of an inconvenience.

¤ ¤ ¤

The casting was nearly finished. Joe had his headliners and his crew. There were some able local actors who had auditioned, and one of the most promising, Susan Dickenson, had become suddenly unavailable. She was summoned by her brother in Bar Harbor, Maine, when their mother had fallen and was in critical condition in the ICU. She flew out immediately without even calling Joe. Her husband, Ted, delivered the bad news. Joe, of course, understood. But there was only one person among the locals who he thought might be able to do an adequate job with Miss Peacock—a crew member, Marilyn Horneby. He asked Marilyn the previous afternoon and while she said she might have preferred the behind-the-scenes work, she was honored to have been asked and would be happy to take it on.

Chapter 6 – Infidelity

Marilyn Horneby had lived on the Cape for most of her adult life. Born Marilyn Mello in Newport, Rhode Island, her grandparents emigrated there from the Azores in the early twentieth century. She met her college sweetheart, Jim Horneby, at the University of Rhode Island twenty-five years before. They married right after graduation, though neither of their parents approved. Jim was certainly not one of the Newport elite, but his family was upper middle class while Marilyn's family struggled to gain a solid working class footing in the community. Despite its reputation as a playground for the rich, Newport at that time was made up of an unbalanced class system that unfairly separated the Portuguese, blacks and white social climbers. The really wealthy were rarely there and were out of touch with the rest of the town. When Marilyn and Jim married, there had been very little intermingling of those classes in Newport, and it was frowned upon. At the more egalitarian ground of URI, however, they were both active in their fraternity and sorority and class distinctions were quickly forgotten. After graduation they continued to be active in the alumni associations for both URI and the fraternal/sororal organizations, attending reunions religiously.

Jim was a pharmaceutical salesman whose territory encompassed southern New Hampshire, all of Massachusetts, the eastern half of Connecticut and all of Rhode Island. Since they knew that he would be traveling a lot, they made Cape Cod their home base. It was centrally located and still small enough to be a nice place to raise children. Marilyn had worked at Cape Cod Community College as an assistant to the President where she helped to increase enrollment 30 percent. After the birth of their children, Emily and Noel, she stayed home. Now that the kids were grown with children of their own and had moved away, Marilyn busied herself with community events, volunteering and her quilting circle.

During the warm weather Marilyn was captain of the local women's tennis team. She was an excellent player and her team won consistently. They were good enough to have played in the regional matches and were hoping to make it to the east coast semi-finals the following year—especially since they were to be held in the winter in lovely Naples, Florida. She had accepted the captaincy without really comprehending the implications. It turned out she was the captain, the mama bear, and the team therapist/mediator all rolled into one. At least once a week she would get a call from someone on the team complaining about someone else.

"Marilyn, please don't pair me with Mary again this week. I simply can't stand to even be in the same room with her, much less on the same side of the net! Just the other day she...blah, blah, blah."

Marilyn usually was able to rearrange the matches to ensure there were no assaults, or worse yet, murders on the tennis court. But the stress of having to manage such petty bickering was sometimes overwhelming. In order to keep her mind clear and sort out who was playing with whom, she took daily walks along the beach. As with everyone within a two-mile radius, she was usually joined on her walks by Casey, the Dickenson's golden retriever. At low tide she often took a circular route, walking down the beach from her house past several summer rental homes, some of which went unused in both winter and most of the summer, down past the Putnam house to Jakes Pond and then back to her house. Her walk of about two miles took her across Jakes Pond and Onion Bay at low tide, though usually in only one direction as they filled back in very quickly. More than once she had seen folks from away swimming back to shore when they got stranded on the outer sandbars of these tidal inlets.

Marilyn and Jim had a beautiful house-
-perfect in every way. It was spacious and
modern with a view to the sea from the entire
back of the house. Marilyn loved to describe
the work they had done making it ready for a
piece in Architectural Digest should that ever
happen. Jim liked house projects and was a
terrific DIY guy. Marilyn watched HGTV to
get ideas for their home and her latest project
was to put a hot tub on the ocean side deck.
Jim protested, claiming it was too hot in the
summer and way too cold and windy in the
winter. However, Marilyn thought the hot
tub would pay off in the end by reviving some
of their early passion. They were still in love,
but Jim seemed a bit distracted lately. And
she thought that some of his sales trips had
been longer than usual.

Marilyn was a striking redhead with a
lithe athletic build. She dressed stylishly and
expensively and she was noticed wherever she
went. Jim had always been indulgent and
never made her feel as though she had
overspent on a dress or a pair of shoes.
Recently, however, he had a tantrum when
she showed off her new Gucci handbag and
lovely Manolo boots. She was puzzled at his
odd behavior, but passed it off as the stress of
his job.

¤ ¤ ¤

On Monday Marilyn started out on her daily walk a little later than usual. Casey joined her soon after she picked up a walking stick that he expected her to throw for him.

"Well, hello, Casey," said Marilyn. There was something about that dog that made it seem natural to speak to him.

"I'm off on my regular route—heading for Jakes Pond. You're welcome to join me, kind sir," said Marilyn, leaning over to scratch his chin.

Casey cocked his head as if he understood or was asking for further explanation.

¤ ¤ ¤

She was a little distracted on her walk as she was ruminating about what she would say that evening at her fundraising gala. She was chair of a committee responsible for the biggest fundraiser on the upper Cape. Sponsored by the Cape Cod Fine Arts Center, Marilyn and her committee were raising funds to enrich the music department of the Upper Cape Regional High School. Marilyn's mother's closest friend had been a piano teacher and inspired Marilyn to appreciate good music. She felt the youth of the Cape deserved every opportunity to do the same. Three of last year's graduates had even gone on to Berklee College of Music, which gave her great satisfaction and fueled her fundraising efforts.

One of Marilyn's greatest luxuries was season tickets to the Boston Symphony Orchestra. She generally spent two nights at The Inn at St. Botolph's. Music transported her to a separate place in her soul where she felt totally alone and whole at the same time. It was something she had never shared with Jim. Even if she had been able to articulate her feelings—as they were just as much unconscious as conscious--she was proprietary about them and kept them private. She vowed many times that she would give up any other luxuries before she would give up her subscription to the Symphony performances. She also used the time in Boston to walk and read and visit those places Jim didn't really enjoy. She had another friend on the Cape with a season ticket, and they would sometimes meet for dinner when her friend's husband didn't attend a concert.

Marilyn left home soon after returning from her walk to be on time for her mani-pedi. She wanted to make sure she looked good for the evening's affair, and by eleven thirty her pedicure was finished and her fingertips were soaking. "It's so nice to relax and get pampered for a few minutes, Thuan. It's been a hectic couple of months getting this event organized. Let's go for the bright red, just for fun!" Thuan got a bottle of "Kiss the Cook" from the shelf, agreeing that red would be perfect for the gala.

Thuan Pham had been doing her nails for several years. Marilyn felt some real fondness for her. She seemed so vulnerable-- young, petite and delicate—nothing like Marilyn who, though very beautiful--tall, with flaming red curly hair, was the antithesis of Thuan. Lovely to look at and engaging to talk to, Thuan's English was fluent and virtually accentless. She had escaped Vietnam with her parents when she was an infant and lived in a refugee camp until she was five. After a transitional location in the United States, her family settled on Cape Cod. She was married to a Vietnamese man several years her senior and they had two children. When she and her husband began to disagree about how the children should be raised and how they should live their lives, it was clear that their age difference and cultural background were problems. When she failed to succumb to his wishes with respect to the children, he surreptitiously took them to Vietnam where he wanted them to be raised; and she did not have the resources necessary to fight for their return. She had no intention of moving to Vietnam, and somehow she survived the loss and moved on with her life. She took some classes at Cape Cod Community College in order to improve her lot in life, but she seemed comfortable as a manicurist. She continued her self-education, though, and was an avid reader. Marilyn would take her books she had enjoyed and would have otherwise donated to the church's fundraising bookstore, and Thuan read them with great enthusiasm. Marilyn had even convinced Jim to get a pedicure last year with Thuan. Lots of husbands of the salon's clientele had given in to their wives' pleas to do something about their ugly feet though they insisted on having it done in one of the private rooms so no one would see them.

While Thuan was doing her nails that day, they exchanged casual conversation about what had occurred since the last time Marilyn was at the salon.

"Did you have a good time in Boston last weekend?" asked Thuan.

"Oh yes," replied Marilyn. "The concert was absolutely awe inspiring. And then, of course, I couldn't resist a bit of shopping on Newbury Street and a great walk along Commonwealth. I even got in some window shopping along Beacon. Do you get up to Boston often Thuan?"

"Not too often, but I was treated to a weekend at the Parker House a while ago."

"Wow, how nice! Sounds like you're being wooed by someone special!"

Thuan went quiet to focus on finishing the nail varnish without chatting. Marilyn's manicure completed, she left the salon to pick up her little black dress and Jim's tuxedo at the dry cleaner's on her way home to prepare some notes for the evening. Back in the car, she found herself returning to the conversation with Thuan about her weekend in Boston and tried to recall having ever mentioned it to her. She could only conclude that she had forgotten and moved the thought to the recesses of her consciousness.

Jim was home when she returned from her errands. She found him beneath the deck overhang cleaning the barbecue that he had just pulled out from underneath. Marilyn stepped out and said, "I picked up your tux for tonight."

Jim looked up at her shielding his eyes from the bright sunlight and said, "What's tonight?"

"It's the music program fundraiser. Don't tell me you forgot?" she remarked accusingly.

"Sorry. My mind was somewhere else. Of course I remember."

"OK. Well, we have to leave here by five fifteen. There are some last-minute things I need to do. And anyway, I want to check on the caterers and the lay-out and such."

71

"Sure. You know, maybe we should take separate cars. I can finish up what I'm doing here and get ready and be there by, ah, what time does it start?"

"Six o'clock, honey. And I'd really like you to be on time."

"No problem. I'll be there in plenty of time."

"OK. I have to get organized and then get ready myself."

"OK."

Jim had returned to his putzing and Marilyn went upstairs to lay out her clothes and accessories and spend some time gathering her thoughts. Again, she found herself harking back to the conversation with Thuan about her Boston trip and thought, 'When could we have talked about that? I just can't figure it out. Oh, well. I've got other fish to fry.' She drew herself back to her notes to be ready.

Marilyn showered and fixed her face and hair. She put on her dress and reached over to get a bracelet out of her jewelry box. She overreached a little and somehow turned her ankle, losing her balance. She pushed the box off the dresser and it plummeted to the floor, jewelry flying everywhere. Cursing her clumsiness, she went down on her knees to gather things up. 'Some of the pieces are way under the dresser, for crying out loud,' she thought to herself. She had to put her face down on the carpet and run her hand underneath. She pulled out what was there to put back into the box and noticed she had picked up an unfamiliar necklace. It didn't belong to her and, in fact, was much too delicate for her wardrobe. Her jewelry made a bold statement, and while it was never gaudy, it didn't hide from view. This one had a finely braided gold chain with what looked like a hand-wrought clasp with an inset good-sized diamond and two delicate little hand-hammered gold pendants—one a sun and the other a moon--with large carat diamonds scattered artfully in both pieces. It was, in fact, unique and extraordinary.

She was perplexed about the necklace and wondered if it could have belonged to her daughter. But she knew that was unlikely as her daughter had inherited Marilyn's height, athleticism and hair. She wore jewelry only under duress and preferred her appendages naked. Marilyn looked at the necklace a little more closely and thought it looked familiar. She left it on the dresser to sort out later.

¤ ¤ ¤

Bertha Poppe was really angry. She had just attended the yearly fundraising gala for the high school music program. Bertha was a regular in the local theatre company and she already had secured a part in *Clue*, so she was eager to get acquainted with the Master of Ceremonies, Rhys Traynor.

The evening started out as she had expected with a lovely cocktail hour and dinner. Things began to fall apart when Traynor got up to begin his keynote address. He immediately made some snide remarks, mocking the President and challenging his competence. Bertha considered the comments inappropriate for the venue and irrationally took them as a personal insult against her. She had been a supporter from the very beginning of the President's campaign and throughout his term of office so far. She nursed her wine while trying to talk herself out of what she had heard, hoping that she had misunderstood Traynor's remarks. She looked forward to working with him and wanted them to work well together. But with each sip of wine, it became more and more difficult to deny that he had said what she thought she heard. Traynor continued to take pot shots at the President, decrying the state of the country since the Democrats had taken over. 'How dare he,' thought Bertha, 'when it was the previous Republican administration that had gotten the country into this mess in the first place!'

Rehearsals for Retribution

By the end of the evening, Bertha had had more wine than she should have and had worked herself into an irrational rage. When given the opportunity to introduce herself, she segued from her introduction as a cast member in the play right into Traynor's misinformation. He was somewhat taken aback by her accusations and excused himself, moving to talk with another fan.

Bertha responded under her breath, but not so discreetly as to be truly speaking to herself, "Despicable pig!" She stomped away in the direction of the women's room where she had to sit down to collect herself.

Bertha had a reputation as a bit of a liberal extremist. She never took kindly to criticism of her beloved Democratic party. Because of her hot temper, she was asked to leave her book club, the local Democratic caucus and even to take a break from her church's Social Responsibility Committee, despite its pursuit of causes very much in alignment with hers. She was hard to like, never mind love.

The occasion for politics had not come up in the theatre group so far, but that was likely to change. Bertha was perfect for the role of the maid in Clue. Putnam originally planned to cast someone tall and lithe with blond sweeping hair and a sweet little voice. But when Bertha read for the role, he rethought his plan. He warmed to the idea of someone small and buxom, brunette and not so much sweet as bossy. He hired her on the spot. Regrettably, he failed to check with other locals about her ability to take direction.

Rehearsals were starting the next day, and Bertha spent some time preparing for her first scene with Traynor. She would not soon forget his public insults and chauvinism, and she would make sure he didn't forget them either!

¤ ¤ ¤

Marilyn's fundraising evening was a smashing success. The room looked glorious, the food catered by Thyme Out was excellent, and the school musicians performed well enough to clear up anyone's doubts about their generous donations. Rhys Traynor did an excellent job as emcee. But for his partisan comments about the current administration, he was clever, dashing and audibly well-received. The guests included all the people she wanted there—local writers, musicians, artists, artisans, actors, business people, political figures. They bid generously knowing that the funds would go directly to the school music fund. Marilyn's speechifying came off without any embarrassment and, in fact, received great applause, which left her having to struggle to contain her feelings of hubris.

The great disappointment—no, irritation--of the evening was Jim's failure to show up. He sent a text message around eight thirty saying he had fallen asleep right after his shower and had slept through everything. He apologized, but that didn't begin to make it all right. She put those feelings on hold, and they only flared up when occasionally someone asked where Jim was. She graciously made excuses, but they were hollow sentiments.

At the end of the evening, Marilyn and her colleagues summed up the evening's take and realized that they had grossed almost $75,000. After expenses, they would net about $65,000 for the music program. Though Marilyn was effusive about the success, she was not able to let go of her feelings about Jim's no-show. When she arrived home, Jim was contrite about having missed the event. He met her at the door with a cognac, which she eagerly accepted but not without pursing her lips in great disdain at his having been so thoughtless as to have missed the occasion.

She said nothing and retreated to the kitchen where she donned an apron over her evening clothes and began banging dishes around in the sink thinking, 'Here I am doing more dirty work on top of all that I did in preparation for and executing the most important community fundraiser of the season while you nap and loll about with your nose in a book!' Jim wisely stayed in the living room quietly reading his book and nursing his cognac. After cleaning the kitchen, Marilyn climbed the stairs to the bedroom and slammed the door behind her. She shed her clothes, put on her most impenetrable pajamas and got into bed. Jim fell asleep with the book in his lap and never made it upstairs to bed.

Chapter 7 – Betrayal

After a fitful night, Marilyn awoke and persuaded herself to greet the day with satisfaction over her success at the fundraising gala. She got ready to meet with her committee to debrief and not to focus on her husband. She set about having breakfast on the deck where she could read the paper in her bathrobe and enjoy her coffee with the quiet of the day. She noticed that the mysterious necklace was missing from the dresser when she looked that morning. Thinking it curious, she had other things on her mind.

After breakfast, she went back upstairs to shower and dress. Her committee was having their meeting over lunch at Lawson's as a treat for having been so successful. She didn't have to be there until noon and decided to do a load of laundry to get ahead of the game. She sorted through Jim's clothes knowing that he was back on the road the following day to spend a few days in Burlington. One thing she didn't want was to have someone think he had an incompetent or uncaring wife who would let her husband go on the road with soiled, stained or wrinkled clothes.

While looking through Jim's clothes to make sure she pretreated any stains, she noticed that he had used more shirts than normal since the last time she did the laundry. She couldn't imagine why he had worn so many. With a load in the washer and another one waiting, she turned to leave the room and awkwardly rammed her hand into the door edge, breaking a nail. Cursing to herself, she decided to leave a little early instead of waiting for that load to finish and make a run by the salon to see if Thuan was available to fix her nail. After all, she didn't want to show up for her "victory" meeting looking shabby after having looked so perfect the night before.

Thuan greeted her warmly and showed her to her regular table. She had another customer on her schedule who was late for her appointment, freeing up a little time for a "fix-it" manicure. Marilyn was effusive in describing the gala event of the night before, and Thuan was an eager listener. Just as she was getting up to sit under the drying lamp, Thuan leaned over to get Marilyn's purse and keys to carry them so Marilyn wouldn't ruin her polish. Hidden a little under Thuan's blouse, her necklace peeked out and Marilyn recognized it.

"Oh. Your necklace. It's just like the one I found yesterday," said Marilyn.

Thuan's hand shot to her neck in response as panic filled her face. In an instant Marilyn understood that it was the very one from her dresser.

"It's your necklace," emerged from her lips--the simple truth spoken almost like an inaudible thought.

Picking up her purse and keys, Marilyn fled the salon. 'Everything is clear now. Jim's emotional distance, frequent absences, more laundry than usual, even why he didn't come to my gala. How could he and how could she! How dare they!' She got into her car, too shocked, stunned really, to do anything. She wanted to scream, to cry, to do something, but instead she sat in stony silence staring at the salon doors.

Her trance was broken when someone's car alarm was triggered and she looked at her watch. 'Damn. I'm supposed to be at Lawson's in ten minutes. Maybe I should cancel,' she thought. 'I can't possibly go. But then, if I don't. . .'

She wasn't sure which was worse--the infidelity or the embarrassment. She suspected that Jim had the occasional fling on the road, but this! Right here in Falmouth! With her manicurist! She worked herself into a fury and decided to go to the luncheon with her head held high.

¤ ¤ ¤

As luck would have it, Brittany got Rhys Traynor's table during the lunch service. She could see that he had closed the menu and put it down. As instructed by the 'Major General,' that was the signal that the customer was ready to order. She approached the table and introduced herself, spieling off the specials and asking what he would like to eat.

"Not so fast, young lady. While I'm hungry, I'm not so hungry that I can't hear those again."

"Oh. Sorry. Sure." And Brittany did it again.

"Has anyone ever told you, dear, that you have lovely diction."

"No, sir. I don't think so. And thanks."

"Brilliant. Now to my lunch. I think I'll have the scallops. . ."

Brittany went to put in the order, thinking he was sweet even if he was sort of old.

¤ ¤ ¤

Marilyn walked into the restaurant late and spotted her friends at the far table near the window. They were always there for her—especially her closest friend, Katrina Allen. Katrina had called her Mimi ever since

Katrina's daughter couldn't say Marilyn's name. The nickname was reserved only for Katrina, though sometimes others used it thinking it would bring them into her circle of friends. Instead, it rankled her. Katrina grew up in Maine and moved to Cape Cod where she and her husband--both trained as marine biologists--worked at Woods Hole Oceanographic Institute. After she became pregnant with their first child, she and her husband decided that raising their children in a nurturing household with a parent at home was much more important that any work at the Institute. Though her husband was very happy to defer to Katrina's career and stay at home, she realized as her pregnancy progressed, that she wanted a life with her children. She had never regretted it.

Jane Tapp had a family therapy practice in Hyannis and had known Marilyn since she and Jim first moved to the Cape. Their children were the same ages and genders and had played together from their infancy and into their college years. Jane loved working with Marilyn on projects where she could contribute without having to take the lead. Marilyn was a brilliant organizer. She knew how to use volunteers and was skilled at making sure the job was done properly without actually having to do all the work herself. Jane was happy to be a worker bee as her family practice took a certain kind of attention that would have distracted her from pulling off the kind of fundraising efforts that Marilyn succeeded in doing.

Judith Parker had grown up in the home of her grandfather in Manhattan. He was a jazz musician during Harlem's heyday and had seen enough success to propel himself into real estate bordering on Central Park. Judith and her family summered on Martha's Vineyard, and after seeing some success as a journalist, she purchased a home on the Cape where she could continue to write without the complication of family and the pace of New York. She met Marilyn in a book group and liked her openness and candor. They were unlikely friends, but their friendship had persisted—for which they were both grateful.

Marilyn convinced these friends to take up tennis and they were now members of her team.

Marilyn motioned offhandedly to the hostess that she would join her friends. She arrived at the table breathless and somewhat disheveled.

"Sorry I'm so late. But I'm here now," said Marilyn.

Katrina said, "Mimi! What the hell happened? You look absolutely wasted."

At that, Marilyn sat down heavily in the chair and, forgetting her resolve about holding her head high, dissolved in tears. "I don't know if I'm more hurt or mad. I guess a lot of both," she said.

She looked up and saw that her friends were gaping at her open-mouthed and stunned. The waitress came over to offer Marilyn a menu, stopping dead in her tracks when Marilyn looked up. She murmured, "I'll come back," and backed away from the table to retreat to another customer.

"Oh, no," called out Katrina, motioning her back to the table. "We'd like very dry gin martinis all around, please, one with a twist and the others olives. And quickly."

"Yes, ma'am," said the waitress turning to go.

"And there may be a second round." Katrina muttered.

The ladies watched her walk away, then all turned as one toward Marilyn who said, "I'm so sorry. I'm so mad, I could spit. But I know this meeting was to talk about our event and here I am spoiling it all."

Katrina said, "No, Mimi. You come first. "Hey, we can reschedule that meeting."

Marilyn touched her hand to her forehead and closed her eyes. She blew out through her pursed lips and with her eyes still closed, said, "Thank you. All of you."

Katrina's hand reached over to cover hers and said, "Y'know, Mimi. How 'bout you take it a step at a time."

Marilyn looked up and began, "When I was getting ready for the auction, I found a necklace on the floor. It wasn't one that I'd ever seen and didn't seem like Emily's style. I left it on the dresser thinking I'd figure it out later. And then Jim didn't show up last night, you know?" She looked around the table to see nodding heads and concerned looks. "He told me he'd taken a nap and slept through it. Yeah right," she said sarcastically.

"This morning, I noticed the necklace was gone. I just didn't really think too much about it, and when I was doing the laundry, I broke a nail. Since I wanted this lunch to be perfect," she sighed deeply and continued, "I went in to have a fix-it manicure with Thuan.

"Thuan. You know her, don't you?" Again, heads were nodding. After all she had recommended Thuan to all her friends.

The waitress returned with their drinks, passed them around, and began to say, "Are you ready to order," when Katrina shot her quite the look, and the waitress said—again, "I'll come back then." She turned to leave while Katrina focused her attention back on her friends. They all eagerly sipped at their drinks.

"When Thuan got up to help me to the drying table, I noticed the necklace around her neck." The others gasped. Their hands went to their mouths and their eyes opened wide.

"You don't mean the necklace from your dresser?" said Judith.

Marilyn nodded wordlessly.

"All I could say was, 'The necklace is yours.'"

"And what happened then?" asked Katrina eagerly. "What'd she do?"

"She dropped my purse and keys on the floor and said nothing. Then I picked up my stuff and headed out the door. I didn't even pay," she said with a little giggle—the kind of giggle that comes from emotional exhaustion.

"And now what're you gonna do?" asked Katrina.

"Damned if I know. You've gotta help me out here, guys. I'm not thinking very clearly."

Jane said, "Don't you think you should be direct with Jim about it? Maybe you need to confront him."

"I'm ready for that. And I think I'll tell Thuan's boss about it, too. She should know if one of her girls is taking advantage of my patronage by screwing my husband," said Marilyn with some vitriol in her tone.

"I'm with you on that," said Judith. "You go, girl." She put her hand up and said, "High five all around, ladies." They all tapped each other's palm around the table.

The waitress decided it might be safe to re-enter the acreage around the table and asked again, "Now, ladies, do you think you might like something to eat for lunch?"

"I feel like I could chew nails. But I'll settle for a rare filet mignon. And just to make it clear, I'm picking up the tab. Ladies, order whatever tickles your fancy. We're going to take Jim to the bank."

While the waitress didn't know whether to smile or wince, she opted for bland and simply responded to questions and tried to remember whatever orders came her way.

Chapter 8 – The Tryst

Rhys Traynor just finished a lovely repast of sautéed bay scallops prepared with ginger and citrus, accompanied by butternut squash pasta with a hint of jalapeño heat and followed by a crisp salad of freshly-picked butter lettuce and curls of aged parmesan cheese. He was seated serendipitously in the booth behind the women and overheard the drama. 'Poor woman,' he thought to himself as he glanced at the red-headed victim.

He signed for his meal and sat back to finish his coffee. Just as he finished, the group got up and moved toward the exit. Arriving at the door to the Inn at the same time as Marilyn and her friends, he bumped into her.

"I am so sorry!" he said in his best British accent, reaching his hand gently to catch Marilyn's arm. The friends recognized him and looked at each other in astonishment at being this close to THE Rhys Traynor.

"Oh, that's OK," replied Marilyn, swiping at the smeared mascara on her cheeks.

"Are you OK?" asked Traynor solicitously? "You look so upset! Is there anything I can do to help?"

"No, no. I'm fine. Thanks so much." Marilyn moved in the direction of the door again.

"Oh but at least let me buy you a drink to make up for my clumsiness."

"Well. . ."

"Please. I'd be delighted and. . ."

By this time the other women, sensing that he was not going to pay attention to them, drifted off to their cars, giving Marilyn a little wave as they left.

"Fine. One drink. That's very kind of you, Mr. Traynor."

"Ah, you know me. Well, please call me Rhys. 'Mr. Traynor' just doesn't sound like me."

Marilyn smiled. "Thanks, Rhys. I'd be delighted."

"Wonderful. And what are you drinking? Martini, maybe?"

"Well, yes. How did you know?"

"I can't imagine you drinking anything else," he said teasingly. They retreated back into the Inn and settled into Rhys' quiet booth. Sitting down, he said, "Now, as I originally asked, are you OK? You seem to be a little troubled. Is there anything I can do?"

"Well," said Marilyn, in reply to his question, "You could shoot my no good bastard of a husband for me!"

"Maybe not such a good idea," Rhys answered accompanied by one of his most seductive grins, "but let's try that drink instead, and you can tell me all about it."

"Um, I shouldn't. I have something I've really got to do."

He looked at her kindly, smiling in a fatherly sort of way. He put his hand gently over hers and said, "I'm wondering if this isn't one of those times you should be focusing just on taking time for yourself, my dear."

Marilyn's face softened, and she said, "What the hell! My little errand can wait."

Marilyn told him her sad story. He told her how sorry he was, that men were such cads, that she deserved better. He helped her forget her troubles with another dry martini.

¤ ¤ ¤

Troy was staying at Lawson's so he could be near Traynor. He even managed to wangle a cottage next door. Not averse to spying, when he saw Rhys go into the bar area that day, he didn't hesitated to follow him. Since he was on the Cape and preppy clothing was expected, he thought he would fit in by wearing his lime green shorts with embroidered pink lobsters and a matching pink polo shirt. He found some darling pink flip flops and with his ever-present and stylishly-dressed Yorkie in its matching carrier, he slid into the booth next to Rhys and ordered a cranberry martini both to celebrate and to fit the locale. He convinced himself that he could feel the energy from the next booth and imagined that any minute Rhys would lean over the top of the booth and invite himself into Troy's cozy nest.

Instead all he could hear was the prattle from the women at the table on the other side of the partition from their booths, weeping and whining about someone's husband who had run off with the manicurist. What did they expect? Men were such jerks. Except, of course, his Rhys. Troy felt sorry that Rhys had to listen to these women. He thought about slipping into Rhys' booth himself to save him from them, but decided to wait to hear the end of the women's story. Not that he cared, but it was a good drama, really.

Finally, beside himself with concern for Rhys' torture and about to make his move, the whining women got up to leave. Then just as Troy began to slide along the seat to move to the next booth, Rhys got up and followed the women to the door. After Rhys' collision with the weeper, Troy watched, gaping, as Rhys gently guided her back to his booth.

'It looks like Rhys is making a play for that woman,' thought Troy. 'Probably just perpetuating his reputation as a Casanova. After all, the public expects. And anyway, the press loves it.' From Troy's perspective, it seemed nothing short of a sham. He had no doubt that he would soon have the opportunity to set that to rights.

Troy surreptitiously left his booth and walked away from them to get to the other side where he could casually walk by and chance a peek. They didn't seem to notice him. Soon Marilyn started to slur her words and said to Traynor, "I'm not really feeling so hot. I'd like to get home."

"You poor dear, this has all been quite a shock. Maybe you shouldn't drive just yet. Why don't you come to my cottage and rest on the terrace for a few minutes until you feel a bit more like yourself?"

The combined effect of the martinis and the attention from this charming, handsome man made it easy to agree as she was very unsteady. 'I wish things were clearer,' thought Marilyn. 'I just can't seem to get my arms and legs going together.' She let herself be led to his cottage without more persuasion on his part. The last thing she remembered was being led to the bed.

Having finished his brief reconnoiter, Troy sat heavily on the bench in his booth and slowly slid toward the back. He sat there trying to talk himself out of what he thought he had witnessed while fanning himself and Princess with his napkin—more out of the sense of drama than the necessity for air. After a very short time, he saw Rhys and the woman leave the booth and walk out. She was obviously staggering, and Rhys was holding her up. They disappeared into the afternoon sunshine and Troy tried to put the incident out of his mind, instead choosing to think about how the play rehearsal would roll out the next day. He was really looking forward to that. And, he was sure Rhys was, after all, just acting.

¤ ¤ ¤

Marilyn awoke to find herself naked in the bed; and Rhys, looking freshly showered, was fastening his cufflinks.

Rhys looked over and said, "Ah! Your husband should not have been so hasty with his wandering eye. You are delightful!"

Grabbing the sheet to cover herself, she cried, "What the hell happened?"

Marilyn saw his mouth moving but heard nothing as she tried only to get up and dressed. Without a backward look, she slunk out the door.

¤ ¤ ¤

The lunch shift was over and Madison and Brittany were exhausted. It was a grueling few hours--made all the more so by the presence of actors and their endless drinks. They were still learning the art of waitressing and had faced some unusual challenges, though truth be told, every shift had its challenges.

There also were four women who had their heads together like nattering old ladies gossiping over some indiscretion by someone the girls didn't know and didn't care to know—someone with an odd name. They drank, ordered late and ate little, though when they paid the bill, they left a generous tip. And then when they left, one of them came back with that Rhys Traynor actor guy and stayed for a while longer without ordering anything other than a couple more drinks. Ms. Butler said the girls had to stay while the customers were still there, though they were itching to get to the beach. But all things considered, they had little to complain about—and they got some good tips.

"Anyway, Maddy, we'll be ready for the dinner shift before you know it."

"Yeah," said Madison. "If 'Major General' Butler ever lets us leave breakfast and lunch."

"Ya know, though, lunch had its exciting moments," Brittany said cheerfully.

"We got to serve Rhys Traynor AND Troy Douglas. How lucky was that?"

"And Rhys said I'd be a good actress."

"Rhys? Really," said Madison. "Now you're on a first-name basis? And how does he know that you'd be a good actress?"

"He said I have good diction at least. Did you see that he went off with that woman who was crying?"

"She sure had a lot to drink. She could barely walk."

"I wonder if she knew what she was doing or where she was going. And where did she go anyway?" Brittany mused.

"Probably to his cottage, not that it's any of our business. Right?"

"I guess. And anyway, that Troy Douglas was a little weird. Did you catch him peeking over the top of their booth? And then circling around when I thought he was going to the men's room. What the heck was that about anyway?"

"Maybe he forgot his purse and had to go back," teased Madison.

They laughed.

"We're bad," said Brittany.

"Yeah. Well, who cares? Anyway we need to go find a way to get into that garage and get Dixie out."

"You're right, Brit. Good idea."

◻ ◻ ◻

Inside her garage, Marilyn opened her car door and heard the phone ringing. She left the door ajar and hurried into the kitchen to grab the phone before it stopped ringing.

"Hello," she said breathlessly.

"Mimi! Where the hell have you been? I've been calling for three hours. I had second thoughts about leaving you at Lawson's with Rhys Traynor—especially in such a state. I feel like I really deserted you."

Suddenly losing all resolve, she moaned, "Oh, Trina. I could really use your help right now. Could you come over?"

"I'll be there in ten minutes. Tops."

"Thanks," breathed Marilyn into the phone. "I'll leave the door open. I cannot wait another minute to take a shower." She hung up and sat down heavily in the kitchen suddenly unable to move.

Just as she started upstairs, she heard Jim's car enter the garage. She moved immediately to the door leading to the garage, opened it and glared as Jim got out of the car.

He saw her and froze, about to speak until she stopped him.

"You are not welcome here right now."

"Don't be ridiculous, Marilyn. I live here."

"I don't care where you live. Right now, you're not coming into this house."

"Look, I didn't murder anyone. I might have made a mistake, but all men do something like this at some point in their lives. I'm sorry this whole thing happened, but we can't ignore it. It won't go. . ."

Marilyn interrupted, "Stop. All men do NOT do something like this. And now is not the time. I don't know when that'll be. But it's not now. I really don't want to see your face right at the moment. Please leave or I'm sure we'll both be sorrier than you could ever imagine."

"All right. I'll go. But this is no way to deal with it."

"IT?! I don't even know what IT is. And how would you know how to deal with IT? You think you can just go off and act with impunity and expect IT to work ITself out? Just go, Jim. Go."

'Gawd. Can I be so self-righteous? I wish I could be sure!' she said to herself as she slammed the door to the garage.

He backed into his seat through the open car door, slammed it and threw the car into reverse, racing back out of the driveway, skidding as he stopped at the street and tore off.

Marilyn unlocked the front door and headed upstairs where she stood under a stream of scalding water. After several minutes, Katrina knocked on the bathroom door and opened it to find Marilyn wrapped in a towel with her head in her hands.

"Mimi! What happened?"

Marilyn looked up numbly and mumbled, "I'm o.k. But I think I'm pretty hung over. I haven't felt this bad since I was in college."

"Well you have every right. Let's go make some tea. Or do you want me to bring it up here?"

"No, I'll come down."

Marilyn let herself be guided by Katrina carefully down the stairs and into the kitchen where she was made to sit down. Once seated, she let it all go.

"Oh, Trina. I don't know. I just don't." She put her face in her hands and sobbed while Katrina approached her and put her hands on her shoulders.

She leaned down and said, "Mimi. We'll figure this out. Together. OK?"

Marilyn looked up and said, "I'm not sure. I'm really not."

"I'll get you some tea and we can talk." She began to fuss with the stove and the sink. She had clearly spent lots of time in Marilyn's kitchen.

Marilyn calmed a little and numbly watched without really seeing anything. Katrina came to the table with sugar and milk, poured the tea in the cups and doctored it up for Marilyn. Too hot to drink, they both picked up the cups and blew across the top until they could sip.

"OK, Mimi. Why don't you start at the beginning—whatever the beginning means for you. I saw Jim turn onto Pinetree Road as I was coming this way. He seemed pretty intent behind the wheel. And a little careless, I thought. So I figured you had words. And anyway, I presume we have the house to ourselves for a while."

Marilyn nodded, took another sip and began, "You know the story of Jim. I don't have much more to say about that now. But Rhys Traynor. . ."

"Rhys Traynor? What about him?"

"I don't know where to begin. I feel so cheap."

"Oh my god, Mimi. What the hell happened?"

She looked down at her hands, fussing with her wedding ring.

"Take your time. I'm in no hurry. Take it easy," Katrina said, reaching across the space between them to softly touch her hand and distract her from her ring.

"After you left, he invited me for a drink."

"And. . .?"

She put her palm on her forehead and leaned into it, then looked up and said, "Trina, I went to bed with him!"

Katrina's hand cupped over her mouth as she audibly sucked in her breath, exhorting, "Mimi! You're kidding, wow? So, was it worth it?"

"I don't know! Anyway, after you left, he invited me for a drink in the bar. At some point, I felt sick and wanted to leave. But he suggested that I go to rest in his room."

"Did he force you?"

"Oh no, I don't think so. I don't remember very much after what I just said. Until I woke up there in his bed."

"Oh jeez, Mimi. "

"This is just between you and me, Trina. OK?"

"Sure, of course. I won't mention it to anybody else. I promise."

"I wish I remembered. What a waste!"

"Are you going to see him again? Did you make plans?"

"No, no Trina. I was so embarrassed I just left as quickly as I could."

"Didn't you say you had a part in the play he's here to do?"

"Yes. I'm Miss Peacock, Sue Dickenson got called away at the last minute."

"Well, you'll see him during the play. What is it again?"

"*Clue.* D'you know it?"

"I think so. Isn't it where the butler did it? I mean, isn't that where the expression comes from?"

"I don't think so. But Rhys is Professor Plum. That's the character who was accused of harassing his female students and was in trouble with his school's administrators."

"I don't think he would really have to harass them, though," said Katrina. "He's too perfect."

"I really don't know what to do. What if he asks me out and expects. . .you know?"

Christine Webb-Curtis and Dimity Hammon

Chapter 9 – Family Secrets

Nico and his Uncle Salvatore Denino's lives couldn't have been more different. Sal was five years older than Nico's mother and was the first in their family to immigrate to America in the 1950s. He was barely sixteen when he landed in New York harbor. Right off the boat he was met by a fellow Sicilian who offered to help him out. Since he didn't speak a word of English, he was grateful to his newfound friend. While Sal was completely beholden to this guy, he never thought to question where he was going and what he would be doing there. His new friend promised everything he hoped for in the "new world"··a great place to live, plenty of food and wine, and lots of money. And frosting on the cake, he would be working with other Italians so his mother tongue would work for now.

Sal's dream was to make enough money in America that anyone else in his family could join him in the promised land. His twelve brothers and sisters had lived their entire lives in poverty in a small Sicilian village. Sicily at that time was totally run by the Mafia. They protected their "family" as long as they were obedient and paid their dues. He hoped that most of his brothers and sisters would eventually follow him across the pond.

In the beginning Sal worked in Chicago as a street cleaner. He was a member of the powerful union that represented city street and sanitation workers. The union had strong connections to the mob, which was ruled by Tony (Big Tuna) Accardo. As in Sicily the Chicago mob protected its own who in turn were bound to service and silence by Omertà, the code of honor that is the backbone of the Cosa Nostra. Sal and his union brothers were happy to be protected by the family. It was the only way of life he had ever known in America and, as promised, he was making good money.

Sal knew how to keep his mouth shut. He was strong and smart, and he eventually rose up through the ranks of the Chicago mob to become a capo. That new position gave him more power and unending profits from the mob's drug and prostitution rings. He had become a favorite of Big Tuna when the boss found out that Sal came from the same village as Accardo's father. Sal became a surrogate member of the Don's real family, welcomed into his mansion as if he were family.

Sal was eventually able to send enough money home to Sicily so his family could live their own American dreams. He found jobs for his brothers and his sisters' husbands until he became concerned that he might be putting them in harm's way because of his business. Instead of settling them in Chicago, he decided to move them to the Boston area. Though they protested over having to leave the fancy mob life, Sal didn't give them any choice. When his sister, Abriana, arrived, he sent her directly to Boston where she met and married a regular guy with no connections to the mob. Abriana and her husband ran a small trattoria. They had two kids--a son, Nico, and a daughter, Tea. Nico became a detective with the Boston Police Department while Tea never married and tragically died from breast cancer at thirty-seven. As a teenager, Nico became aware that his uncle had worked in Chicago and may have been involved in some shady business, but he figured his Zio Sal's questionable activities were all in the past.

He figured wrong.

¤ ¤ ¤

As soon as Sal felt comfortable that he had a relatively secure position with the Chicago mob, he bought a modest house on Thatcher Avenue, a few blocks away from Tony Accardo's in River Forest. The house was unassuming, but it had a few attributes that made it perfect for Sal. It had a huge backyard where Sal could have an ample garden. Every summer he grew several different kinds of tomatoes, lettuce and other greens, squash, artichokes, lots of herbs and any other vegetables that struck his fancy. He also had several fruit trees. As a true Italian, Sal didn't like food that wasn't absolutely fresh and he didn't like other people touching his food. He also had a few chickens and would have had a pig or a cow if that had been allowed. The neighbors weren't so hot on him slaughtering the chickens in the backyard, but they knew whom he worked for and didn't dare complain.

After having grown up with all his siblings in a very small house, he just liked having a big house all to himself. He loved the spacious screened-in sleeping porch on the second floor overlooking the backyard and slept out there from spring through late fall. The small front porch looked out on the forest preserve where he watched the seasons change.

The house was built before the turn of the century. The small detached garage had been used originally for a buggy. Sal eventually replaced his small American car with a Ferrari--his only indulgence. Because he didn't want to draw attention to himself, he kept it in the garage, taking it out mostly at night and outside the city.

Of course the best thing about his house was that it was within easy walking distance of Tony's home so that Sal could be there in a few minutes when bidden.

Sal hoped that one day, when his nephew came around to his side, he could have his family all together in this house, cooking and eating and enjoying la bella vita.

¤ ¤ ¤

Members of the Indian tribe on the Mosquito Coast of Nicaragua supported themselves and their families by diving for lobster tails, which were then sent to the United States. The demand was huge, but diving for the elusive lobster was hard and dangerous work. Most of the divers had suffered severe disabilities from diving too deep using inadequate equipment, which was all they could afford, and then having to come to the surface too quickly, resulting in too much nitrogen pooling in their system. This syndrome was known as the bends and usually resulted in partial, if not full paralysis and often, death. Despite the danger the Mosquitos loved diving for lobster.

These people were miserably poor and had no other way to support their families until the drug lords realized that such isolated and needy folks were prime candidates as collaborators in the drug trade. The Indians didn't know how much money was involved. They were grateful to take the pittance offered to run drugs up the coast.

The hitch had been that once the drugs reached Teguchegulpa, there were few ways to continue the cocaine's voyage to the east coast of the states where they could be distributed.

That was until Sal heard the story about the Mosquito Indians and their lobster tails. Sal came up with a foolproof plan.

Normally, once the divers caught the lobsters they would detach the tail, where all the meat was and sealed them in heavy plastic bags. They would be loaded onto cargo ships, which traveled up the coast to various ports, then offloaded and distributed to markets all across the United States. Sal figured that it wouldn't take much money to get a few of the natives who were already involved in dangerous drug running to take the meat out of the tails and substitute cocaine. Once those tails were packaged and sealed, they would be included with the rest of the shipment to an east coast port. Sal just made sure that they would all go to Boston where he had friends on the docks who would be happy to help him out--for a fee. Because the tails were sealed and the lobster was a bit smelly, the shipments could get past the sniffer dogs with ease.

Sal saw his plan as a sort of community aid project to improve the divers' lives since they would be able to buy better equipment with the extra money. They could still do what they loved but without the adverse consequences. Even better, the families would all benefit because the men did not become disabled. Sal was quite proud of himself. He had never thought of himself as a do-gooder, but now wished he could tell the world what a benevolent fellow he had become. Of course, he was making too much money and having too much fun to share his scheme with others!

¤ ¤ ¤

Francis McCormack was not a nice guy. Nico had always believed that it was Francis who was behind the whole dirty drug deal that had landed Francis' brother, Charlie, in prison and Nico under suspicion of disloyalty to his colleagues on the force. Francis would never forget or forgive Nico for not only having led the investigation, but for having exposed the culprits, including his own brother.

Unfortunately, Francis and poor Charlie were not the only ones who were unhappy with the outcome of the case. Those exposed drug deals had widespread connections--not the least of which was the Chicago mob. And anything involving the Chicago mob still involved Nico's Uncle Sal even though Nico was innocently unaware that his uncle was anything other than a has-been gangster from ancient history.

Salvatore Denino was still very much a part of the mob scene and was specifically interested in Boston where the market for hard drugs was thriving. Though there were few cops willing to help out since Charlie's imprisonment, it was relatively easy to run supplies by boat along the coast with impunity. He had a good business going-- bringing cocaine up from Colombia in cargo ships that, for the most part, carried legitimate goods. He was able to use some of those legitimate goods to smuggle his cocaine. Once the ships came into port in Boston the drugs were off-loaded under cover of darkness and loaded onto one of the small pleasure crafts that were common out in the harbor at any time of day or night. At the dock, independent laborers did the transfer. These were laborers who worked by the hour and didn't care what the cargo was or why it was always unloaded at such odd hours. The Boston mafia considered these activities small potatoes and were happy to look the other way as, it seemed, were the police. He had a partner, Francis McCormick, with connections on the force. The drugs were then taken down the coast to caches on the Cape or in the small town of Mattapoisett on the mainland where they were further distributed.

Frances had been charged with finding someone to be the middle man in this drug scheme he was running with Sal. He didn't want the usual petty criminal who would be easily noticed on the Cape. Instead he wanted a person or two who needed money, but would be considered respectable by the community.

While Nico was unaware of his uncle's continuing activity, Sal was absolutely aware of what Nico was up to and had plans to make use of the family connection. In Sal's world nothing was more important or stronger than family. He was certain that Nico would cooperate when the family connection was invoked.

He was very, very wrong.

¤ ¤ ¤

In his years as a beat cop and then a detective, the one thing that Nico knew connected crime, misery and death was drugs. He came to hate the drug business and those who peddled them to anyone, especially children. Having been addicted to cigarettes for years, he fully understood how easily people could become addicted to hard drugs and how much fortitude and support it took to break the habit. And he understood that it was usually drugs that led to other crimes, both petty and serious. Nico was a first generation Italian American, however, and had no illusions about the connection between the Italian American community and crime with drugs in particular. He had sworn to do everything in his power to defeat the drug lords in his jurisdiction. The most recent result of his campaign had been the trial and conviction of Charlie McCormack and Nico's subsequent shunning by much of the rest of the department.

While Nico thought his family connection to an old member of the Chicago mob was unimportant to him or his family, Chief Gerry Walsh, his boss at Boston PD, knew better. He learned about Nico's Uncle Sal when Nico joined the force many years before, but Nico was unaware that the Chief knew or cared anything about his family. He followed Nico's career as a beat cop and was very careful to make sure he was not only completely clean, but had no knowledge of his uncle's current connections. He would have sworn on his life that Nico would arrest his uncle in a heartbeat if he had discovered him doing anything illegal. He also knew that it was unlikely that Sal Denino would ever be caught with his hands dirty. He was too smart and too well connected to have ever let that happen. But in any case, it would never have anything to do with Nico.

Of that he was sure.

Chapter 10 – Dixie Finds a Friend

Enzo DiSiena was not a thug by choice. Fat as a kid, he was the butt of other kids' jokes. He was basically a gentle, shy, scared guy who would do anything to have the other guys like him. All through his school years, the bullies in his school took full advantage of him to do their dirty work. Even after they all miraculously managed to graduate from high school—thanks to the application of "social promotion," all too often used in public schools, he continued to be sucked into doing their bidding. Though Enzo believed he was part of a really cool gang, he was just an easy stooge whom the other kids described as "strong like bull, smart like tractor."

The gang's handlers convinced them that they were going to have a great summer, smuggling drugs from Boston to a place near Fall River and then over to the Cape. There was a possibility that deliveries would also include Martha's Vineyard and Nantucket. They were provided a very slick, very fast jet boat for their drops, which, in itself, made the venture worthwhile. They pictured themselves tanned and buff on the fancy boat with bikini-clad girls falling all over them. Of course, the reality was that all of the smuggling had to be done at night when it was cold and wet. More often than not they were huddled together in their dark hoodies trying to stay warm while searching for the place they were supposed to drop the stash.

That's where Enzo came in. He was strong enough to get the large bags of cocaine off the boat and into their safe place quickly. The others managed to appear to occupy themselves with some other important chore while he did all the heavy lifting. Enzo never appeared to notice. Anyway, he liked the run from Fall River to Falmouth because the drop in Falmouth was a house. The usual drops were covered holes in the ground where he could encounter all sorts of creepy critters that gave him the shivers just to think about. Here they had to be careful to only use their flashlights, but at least they could stay overnight at the cottage and be warm and dry.

On this particular day everything went smoothly. They were able to maneuver the boat into the tricky bay without much trouble and land by the deserted house without any problem. They quickly offloaded the drugs and got them into the house, thanks to the heavy lifting of Enzo the bull. Then while the other three guys took a break from all their effort, Enzo put the bags in a hiding place in the garage.

Enzo kept hearing a noise in the corner as he went back and forth with the bags. On his last haul, he saw a pretty little tabby cat in the corner. Despite Enzo's tough-guy façade, he loved animals, and when he called to the cat, it came right to him. They had a little chat—he cooing, she purring, and he left her there, hoping that she wasn't trapped. She looked well-fed and healthy—clearly not a stray. But he planned to bring her food and treats when he returned. He decided against telling the other guys about her, thinking they might ridicule him. He gave her a goodbye pat and went back into the house.

"All OK out there, Enzo?" asked Alfonzo, the head thug. "Is everything hidden well enough?"

"All's good," replied Enzo.

"OK, guys. Let's get the boat up. We gotta hunker down to wait for the pick-up."

They pulled the now-lighter boat farther up on the shore and headed back toward the house.

Just as they were heading into the house, a girl came running over from the house next door shrieking.

"Thank god, my cat!" she panted. "My cat's in there and she's gotta be starving and scared. Oh-my-god, please, please help!! She's in the garage and she's probably close to death. We've got to get her out now!"

"Never mind the goddamn cat," growled Alfonzo; but Enzo was already opening the door as he turned to Brittany and said, "That's a nice cat. Is she yours, lady?" Enzo struggled some with the salt-rimed lock.

"Yes, and I'm sure she's scared to death!"

"She was real nice to me, I wanted to feed her, but I didn't have nuthin'."

Enzo stopped short of opening the door and looked back at Brittany. He remembered the lecture he got from Alfonzo. "Don't ever let anyone in the house, stupid," Alfonzo told him over and over.

"Uh, you have to stay here. I'll get your kitty. Just wait, OK? I don't wanna get in trouble."

"Just get outta my way, for cryin' out loud," Brittany said, trying to shove him aside. "I need to get my cat!"

He put his arm across the door to prevent Brittany from entering and said, "I can't, ya see, I'll get into trouble and I don't wanna get into trouble!" Enzo pursed his lips making his chin all wrinkly and his eyebrows tightened.

"Oh, whatever then. Just bring me my cat!"

While Brittany was attempting to rescue Dixie, Madison was surveying the scene. Now that it appeared Dixie would be rescued, she realized that there was something funny going on.

"Hi guys, what's happening?"

"We got lost, ya see? Now we're stuck and we need to get some rest! So get your cat and get the hell outa here!"

"OK, OK. I'll just wait for my friend and we're gone." Madison backed away, looking to see if Brittany was still in sight.

A few minutes later Enzo appeared with Dixie, cooing softly to her.

"Here's your kitty, lady. What's her name?"

"Dixie."

Enzo held her in front of him, turned her around to face him and said, "Can we play next time, Dixie?"

"Sure, sure," barked Brittany. "Just give me my cat!"

She grabbed Dixie and ran for the cottage.

"Bad, kitty," she scolded. "That's the last time you get out!" She put the cat down inside and unperturbed, Dixie headed straight for the food.

¤ ¤ ¤

Josiah and Sam were looking forward to the evening with Madison and Brittany. They finally got there at about nine after a bit of a fiasco with their dinner. Josiah had made the mistake of suggesting Sam cook on his own. He plopped a cookbook in front of him, and left him to it. After about a half hour, Josiah returned to the kitchen where he found Sam frantic for help and dinner barely salvageable. They both knew that Sam needed more help in order to work his way around the kitchen—if working your way around the kitchen meant more than opening a can or cooking up some ramen noodles.

It was already dark when they reached the road to the cottage and it took them a while to identify where it was. They were warned that the porch light was burned out, but they hadn't realized how remote the place was with only one other cottage nearby.

The girls were waiting on the porch when they finally arrived and handed them each a beer. They spent a bit of time catching up and then settled down to gripe about their jobs.

"I can't believe how much work waitressing is," Brittany said. "Like you have to actually memorize the orders. God forbid you should write anything down! And then you need to bring the food all at the right time and not spill anything. . . Crap!"

"You should have to deal with the guys on the golf course!" chimed in Sam. "Some old guy kept complaining that the greens were slow and bumpy when he really was a shit golfer. What a pain in the ass!"

"Aw, come on," said Madison. "We should be happy to have jobs, for cryin' out loud. I can't tell you the number of guys in my dorm that couldn't find anything, and they're really feeling screwed about next year's spending money, never mind tuition."

"Yeah, I know. We're lucky and anyway, look at where we get to work!" said Josiah.

"Hey, enough already," whined Sam. "We brought some more beer. Let's get to 'em!"

A storm had come in and the tide was high. The wind was blowing off the bay toward them--strong but warm and they were quite comfortable on the porch chatting easily about this and that.

Sam looked over to the cottage next door and asked what was going on.

"We're not sure," said Brittany. "But whatever it is we don't think it's good. And that boat is something else."

"Are they in the house?" asked Josiah. "Why're all the lights out?"

"What boat?" said Sam. "And why are you whispering?"

"We don't want 'em to hear us," replied Madison. "They were here today when we got home and..."

"And we had to go over there because Dixie was locked in the garage," Brittany interrupted. "And we couldn't call you guys because you were working so we just went and told them. We got her back, but they weren't very friendly except for the big dumb guy."

"They said they were lost and wanted to get out of there, but that was a couple of hours ago and they're still there." added Madison. "It's all pretty strange. I'd sure like to know what's going on!"

What with the noisy wind and the broken porch light, they were confident that they couldn't be seen or heard. They continued to talk quietly.

"It's probably gonna be up to us to find out. Right, Maddy?" said Brittany. She was very proud of the "detective" skills they had acquired the summer before when they figured they had solved the mystery of who killed Joe Putnam's girlfriend. They admitted that they might have had some help from Detective Forgione, but they still considered themselves to have found the murderer almost single handedly.

Sam and Josiah were around during last summer's mystery and were also questioned as suspects, so they knew that the killer was found by accident and that both the girls and the detective were serendipitously there at the same time the discovery was made. Their "detective" skills consisted mainly of being overly curious--really nosy, but they were not about to contradict either of the girls.

"OK, guys," whispered Brittany. "Let's go see what's going on over there."

"Right." replied Sam snidely. "What are we gonna do? Just stroll on over and ask them what's up?"

"Of course not," scoffed Maddy. "You guys both have on jeans and dark hoodies. We'll get ours and off we go!"

"Whoa," said Josiah, confused. "Whaddya thinking?"

"As long as we're in dark clothes, we'll just sneak over and take a look," said Brittany. "Piece o' cake! We do it all the time at home. You'd be amazed at what you can find out!"

Sam and Josiah looked at each other in amazement. These girls had unexpected tricks up their sleeves, and they seemed to have too much expertise in skulking around. But they were up for an adventure and pulled their hoods over their heads while they waited for the girls to get ready.

"Just follow us. It'll be fine."

A mere three minutes later the girls emerged from their cottage completely dressed in dark clothes and footwear, each carrying a very small flashlight with a concentrated halogen bulb which fit in the kangaroo pockets of their sweatshirts.

"Let's go," said Maddy. "We should try around the back by the garage and see what happens from there."

"Sounds good to me," replied Brittany. "Ready guys?"

The boys had no idea what was going on, but they were willing to go along for the ride and let the girls lead the way. They went out to the road and headed toward the garage doors carefully avoiding the gravel car path.

¤ ¤ ¤

Years ago the girls had found out the hard way that gravel driveways were not only popular for their looks and easy maintenance, but also because they made it hard to sneak up to a house. They misspent some of their teen years sneaking out of their homes and exploring Salem at night just for the fun and excitement. They never did anything wrong or dangerous, but loved the thrill of getting away with it. They were pretty efficient at making themselves invisible. On one of their early midnight outings, Madison's dad, who spent some of his own teenage years on midnight prowls, stealthily followed the girls. He just wanted to make sure the girls were safe–not meeting any boys or worse. After a short while he satisfied himself that all was innocent. He crept back into bed and assured his wife that all was fine.

¤ ¤ ¤

When they got to the far side of the garage, they were able to see the guys moving around inside the house. They appeared to be lugging some bags around.

The kids watched for a while and then snuck back to the cottage, carefully retracing their steps. This time they went into the cottage so they could talk without any fear of being overheard.

"Oh-my-god," said Brittany. "Whaddya think is going on over there?"

"I think it's scary—whatever it is," Maddy answered.

Just then they heard a car pull in behind their cottage and stop next door. They ran to the window in Brittany's room and peered out.

"Hey look, there's a car pulling in at the garage door. It looks like an old Toyota. I can't see what the driver looks like, though," said Sam. "He's got a wool cap pulled way down. And the headlights are off. That cottage is pretty popular."

"Oh well. Maybe it's some friend of those guys," said Josiah. "Let's forget about it."

"OK for now, but we're gonna keep our eyes on the place," said Brittany.

Josiah interjected, "Hey, guys. Why don't you come for dinner tomorrow at our house? Sam's cooking and I know he'd love to show off."

Sam shot Josiah a panicked look.

"Sounds good," Madison nodded and got a reciprocal nod from Brittany.

"Sure. Great idea. What time, then?"

"How about six thirty? I just rented the last Woody Allen movie—*To Rome with Love*. We can watch it after dinner if you're interested."

"Are you kidding?" said Madison. "Somehow we missed it last semester. So, great. We'll see you tomorrow, then."

"Great."

Christine Webb-Curtis and Dimity Hammon

Chapter 11 -- Accusations

Marilyn felt restored after a welcomed dreamless night. She was slightly more comfortable about what happened with Rhys and she found herself thinking about him more and more--how handsome he was and how special he had made her feel—at least the part she remembered. She couldn't get him out of her head. Katrina had stayed the night so Marilyn wouldn't be alone. Her husband was happy to hold down the fort— especially under the circumstances, though Katrina only told him that Jim had had an affair. Marilyn sent Jim a text message that he was not to return home until she was ready to talk. He had the courtesy to reply that he got the message—not that he communicated any remorse. Anyway, he would be out of town for a few days, which gave her the time she needed. Together the friends prepared a lovely dinner and laughed and cried their way through the evening. Katrina had just left for home and Marilyn was ready to make a visit to the salon.

Feeling starry-eyed, Marilyn considered letting Thuan off the hook and laying all the blame on her soon-to-be ex-husband, but dismissed the thought summarily. After all, Thuan was a perfectly willing partner in this affair, and also made out like a bandit with that necklace.

She figured that Thuan wouldn't have lasted any longer than the others. She realized now that she had known about them subliminally, but never admitted to it. Before leaving for the salon, Marilyn went into Jim's study and carefully looked through all of the credit card bills he had so carefully kept—or more truthfully, hoarded. She never really paid attention to their bills since she was able to use her credit cards at any time and for virtually anything she wanted. Jim took care of all the finances. It appeared that his obsession with secrecy about the money was to be his undoing. She not only found the receipt for Thuan's necklace, over $2,000, but on further investigation she found that over several years he had purchased ten baubles of equal value ranging from rings to earrings to necklaces—none of which belonged to Marilyn. The tennis bracelet from two years before cost almost $5,000. She thought that tryst must have been quite something. In addition she found IOUs and receipts from several of the casinos scattered around his sales territory. It looked like Jim had a gambling problem. Clearly she needed to pay attention to her financial situation.

Her discovery stripped Marilyn of any shred of feelings she might have for Jim and she now saw him only as an investment against which she would be drawing large and well-deserved dividends as long as she got her dibs in first. She had already been in touch with a lawyer who advised her to freeze their joint bank accounts. Evidently Jim had underestimated Marilyn enough to never bother to segregate money in another account so that he could draw on it without her knowledge. She had also frozen all the credit cards. She had a good chuckle when she thought about what would happen when Jim discovered that he was unable to pay for his hotel room in the morning.

¤ ¤ ¤

She timed her arrival for the peak of activity with late morning customers. When she walked in, Thuan looked up from her work on a woman's hands and went pale as she saw Marilyn approach the counter and ask for the owner, Kim Janson. Kim was also from Vietnam, like Thuan, and had met a professor at Cape Cod Community College when she was a student there. After graduation they had dated and eventually married. He continued to teach and together, they opened this salon where they hired other Vietnamese women. The shop was not luxurious, but it was very clean and light and airy. It was no "sweat shop." Everyone was treated well—both customers and staff. And the atmosphere was one of ease and comfort.

The receptionist greeted Marilyn warmly and asked if she wanted to see Thuan.

"Will it be a mani, pedi or both today, Mrs. Horneby?" she asked.

"I'm not here to be served," replied Marilyn a little more loudly than usual. "I'd like to speak with Kim, here and now, please!"

Hanh, the receptionist, nervously picked up the phone and called back to her boss. She spoke rapidly in Vietnamese, paused while Kim spoke, and then turned to Marilyn.

"Mrs. Horneby, Kim can speak with you. If you follow me I will show you to her office."

"Not a chance," Marilyn shot back. "I need to see her out here. I think I'd like these other lovely ladies to hear what I have to say."

By now Marilyn had the attention of everyone in the salon, especially Thuan, who was trying to concentrate on her client's manicure with her head down. Thuan knew she had no excuse for her affair with Jim. But he had been so nice to her after her husband left with their children and made her feel so attractive. Lately, though, she sensed that his interest was beginning to wane and suspected he might have moved on to someone else.

Hanh tried again to suggest that Marilyn see Kim in the back office, but she stood her ground. She was almost enjoying this experience, no longer caring that she was the nice responsible woman who volunteered for charities and was considered the perfect citizen. Jim had disabused her of that persona. She was now Marilyn the avenger-- out to right the wrongs heaped on women all over the world! Or, at least, the Cape.

Finally, Kim appeared from her office, her usual self-confidence gone. She sensed that this was going to end badly and couldn't guess why. Surely a bad manicure wouldn't raise this kind of ire?

All of those drama lessons Marilyn took through the local theatre group came back to her as Kim entered the room to step behind the counter. With a burst of emotion she pointed her finger—the one with the repaired nail of the day before--in the direction of Thuan and pronounced, "That woman left her necklace in my bedroom. MY bedroom! She screwed my husband, the bastard, and God knows how many other men in this town."

Marilyn's voice had escalated during the conversation, becoming more and more agitated as she relived the whole experience of yesterday's discovery of the necklace around Thuan's neck. A hush came over the store and everyone—customer and employee—was looking from Marilyn to Thuan and back again. Thuan's hand was at her neck, nervously fingering the necklace.

Kim's hands flattened out on the counter stiffly and she pushed herself back away a little as if the information would be different with a little distance. "What are you saying, Mrs. Horneby?"

She spun around and addressed the other women in the salon. "Ladies, have you brought any of your husbands here for a pedicure in the back room where they wouldn't be embarrased?

"Well, if you have, they might have gotten more than you could imagine! And Kim, don't tell ME that you didn't know anything about this! That woman has to go or you'd better have a pretty good explanation."

In fact, Kim was as shocked as her client at that moment. She recently noticed that Thuan was not spending as much of her free time with the rest of her staff and that she seemed to have more money than usual, but she thought that maybe she was reconciling with her husband and he was trying to woo her with some extra cash. She never suspected for a moment that Thuan was having an affair with one of her best client's husband.

"Kim. What are you going to do?"

"Well," Kim stammered. "If Thuan did have an affair with your husband, I'll have to deal with her. But. . ."

"There's no 'but' about it," Marilyn broke in loudly. "And I don't want to hear that you'll just take care of it. Exactly how many women do you think are going to trust this salon if you let your staff steal their husbands?"

Kim began to speak, but realized the question was rhetorical and didn't really deserve an answer.

"Zero. That's how many."

Turning toward Thuan, Marilyn said, "I never want to see your face again." Marilyn started walking toward her and Kim awkwardly hurried around the counter to make sure she was able to prevent any violence from occurring. Of course Marilyn had no intention of really hurting Thuan. "I actually cared about you," she said pointing at her chest. I felt sorry for you when you lost your kids. I gave you gifts. How could you be so cold as to accept them while screwing my husband!"

Kim went over to Thuan, took her clippers and polish, donned a clean pair of gloves and without a word took over the manicure she had been working on. Thuan left the salon without ever raising her eyes from the floor. Marilyn wheeled around and strode toward the exit. She opened the door, slamming it behind her and walked stiffly to her car, got in and drove out of the parking lot leaving a maelstrom in her wake.

'That takes care of that,' she thought.

¤ ¤ ¤

After Marilyn left the nail salon, those who remained—customers and workers alike—looked around at each other uncomfortably. No one spoke a word—until Lil Forgione spoke up. Lil was in the salon for her quarterly pedicure. Now that she lived on Cape Cod and her toes were available for public view during the summer, she felt it important to look as presentable as possible—especially given her newly-established role in the Catholic community. She had chosen Kennebunkport Red to show off her "racy" side.

"Well that was awkward!" Lil smiled at Kim and the woman sitting in the next chair. "Too bad for both of them. It looks like the person missing from that triangle has made a pretty mess of two women's lives," she nodded to the client in the next chair.

The woman said, "I'll say. And I know him. He's a devilish sort of guy. You know-- attractive, flirtatious, and often on the road."

"Personally, I like to keep my man close to home, if you know what I mean," said Lil. "And monogamous as his wedding vows told him to be." Lil's husband had strayed early in their marriage, so she knew from experience the pain of betrayal. But they worked it out and it never showed its ugly face again. Their marriage wasn't perfect, but in the end, they were still in love and had great respect for each other. So whatever dissension came their way was always resolvable.

Lil thought she could be helpful to the woman who just stormed out of the salon if she were asked, but she knew better than to interfere in such a thing—unless the person involved was a personal friend. She let it go for the moment and enjoyed the remainder of her pedicure.

Christine Webb-Curtis and Dimity Hammon

Chapter 12 – Sam Makes Dinner

"OK, Jos. Can we start again in the kitchen. You offered me up like a human sacrifice yesterday when you said I'd be making dinner. You gonna show me now? No cookbooks either."

"Sure, Sam," said Josiah. "I agree. Let's start fresh."

"Thanks. And you know the girls are going to be here in about forty-five minutes."

"It's OK. In a half hour, we'll be ready to slow down. We can all be in the kitchen as if it were the place where all the action is. And they won't know the difference. 'Kay?"

"Yeah. I guess."

"Let's see what we have here," he said looking in the refrigerator. "It looks like we have some chicken breasts. Work for you?"

"Sure. I'm open to pretty much anything. My mum cooked hamburger in about a thousand different ways when I was growing up. Anything not ground, frankly, works for me."

"OK. How about something simple-- chicken breasts, risotto, and salad?"

"Hell yes. Doesn't sound simple, but tell me what to do. I'm so ready."

"OK, let's see. Get the chicken breasts and rinse 'em off in cold water."

Sam did as instructed.

"Put 'em in this bowl," he said, handing him the bowl.

"And let's add some brandy. It's in the cupboard. I'll get it. There. Now sort of massage the chicken a little with it."

"Like this?"

"Sure. That's fine. And let's put in some garlic. Take one of those cloves over here and put it down flat on the cutting board."

"This way?"

"Yeah. Now take the flat of the blade and smash it."

"Ooh, I like doing this," said Sam.

"And peel it with your fingers, then chop it up. Best way to do that is to rock the blade over the garlic like this." Sam does.

"That's great. Now add it to the chicken and brandy. And grind in some of this black pepper," he said handing him the grinder. "And let's go out into the garden and get some mint."

"Mint? You must be kidding. We're not making candy, are we? Sam said while washing his hands."

"Don't get your knickers in a twist, Sam. Have some faith, for cryin' out loud."

"Sorry. OK. But I don't have a clue what mint looks like."

"Grab those sheers and come with me, then," said Josiah.

Out into the garden they went where Josiah snipped some mint and some basil and picked a few tomatoes. Back in the kitchen, he rinsed them all and placed them in the colander to drain.

"Now the onions."

"These?" asked Sam while showing them to Josiah.

"Yeah. So I'll do one and you can do the other. So we take the skin off the onion and then cut off the stem end."

"OK."

"And then use this knife and cut it in half the long way. . .like this," Josiah said showing Sam how to do it with one of the onions. "Then lay the half on the cutting board and hold it with the palm of your hand. And slice into the onion—like this—parallel to the cutting board," again showing him how to do it.

"I got it," said Sam miming Josiah's actions.

"Hey be careful! That knife is sharp."

"Yow! I'll say. That was close. I don't think I've noticed that before. The knives I grew up with weren't like this."

"That's part of what makes cooking easy," said Josiah. ". . .a sharp knife."

"Awrighty then," said Sam. "I'll be careful."

Sam got the hang of it and chopped the onion without a single bloody incident.

"I put the pan on the burner. See?"

"Yeah. Why that pan?" said Sam.

"'Cause the heat is even and steady. It's the best way to cook something like this. My mum used this pan all the time."

"What is it? It's really heavy."

"It's enameled cast iron. It's good."

"OK. I'll take your word for it, then."

"So add a little olive oil. Yeah, that's fine. And put the onions in there to soften and brown a little."

"Do I need to stir it a lot?"

"In a minute. Get them going first. And now let's do another onion the same way, but finer pieces."

Sam seemed to be getting the hang of it with the knife but got a little sloppy, nearly slicing his finger off.

"Whoa there, Sammy. Leave your fingers to the cabinetmaking. Watch what you're doing and hold the knife here at the shank so you have more control. You know, the way I showed you before."

Sam finished them up and Josiah showed him which pan he wanted to use for the risotto and got some butter to sauté the onions.

"Now let's leave that for a while. When we're ready with everything else, we can start to cook the risotto. It needs a little attention, so you can't be too distracted with everything else," said Josiah.

"So now that the onions are little browned, let's add a little more olive oil and add the chicken breasts. But wipe them off with a paper towel first, Sammy."

"That's right. Just like that," confirmed Josiah. "And we can let that brown on that side. Let's chop up the mint now."

He showed Sam how to roll the leaves up and slice across them to produce little strips. "And set it aside. Here's a little bowl."

"Thanks. OK. Now what?"

"Check the chicken. Here are some tongs. If it's brown on that side, you wanna turn 'em over and brown the other side. . . Yeah, that's right."

"What now?"

"Let's do some vinaigrette. Do you know how to make it?"

"If you don't mean taking the screw top off the bottle, then no. As you know from last night, I don't know how to make much of anything except toast and cereal. And why do you think I came over here happily every time your mother invited me?" Sam grinned impishly. "OK. I can also make a peanut butter and jelly sandwich."

Josiah smiled. "OK, then let's do the vinaigrette. Get the mustard out of the fridge."

"This?" Sam said, holding up the yellow mustard.

"No, no. It's the Dijon. It's in the door. Yeah, right. That's it."

"Put a teaspoon in this bowl. Then add a little vinegar."

"How much?"

"About a coupl'a tablespoons."

"What the hell does that mean?" said Sam?

"Like this. Not very much," demonstrated Josiah. "Stir it up with this whisk. And here's the olive oil. So, pour it in very slowly until it emulsifies."

"Whaddya mean? Emulsifies."

"Whisk it while you're pouring until it begins to thicken."

Sam whisked and the mixture suddenly began to thicken. "Wow! Look at that. That's mega cool."

"Yeah. Now, we can use honey, which is cheaper, or the maple syrup my mum left in the refrigerator when she moved. Either way it's good. Whaddya want?"

"I say use the cheaper stuff if it's all the same."

"Good choice," Josiah said reaching for the honey. "Just squeeze in a dollop—whatever that is."

"Yeah. I have no idea. But here goes. . ."

"Perfect. Stir it in and let's go back to the stove."

Sam said, "This is the coolest stove, Jos. Y'know?"

"Yeah. My mum loves it. Me, too."

145

"So now what?"

"Take the chicken out and put it on this plate here. . . Right. Now let's put in this wine—about a cup."

"Ooh. Look out," said Sam.

"It's fine. You just need to deglaze it."

Blank stare from Sam.

"That just means stirring the bottom to get all the good stuff off."

Blank stare continues.

"I guess you'll just have to trust me, Sammy."

"OK, Jos. I'll do it."

"See? That's it. See how the bottom cleaned off? All the pieces of browning of the chicken are in the juice now. So put the chicken back in and add about half the mint."

"Are you sure?"

"Yeah. Just do it."

¤ ¤ ¤

They were all seated comfortably in the living room with their raspberry sorbet and local gooseberries. Madison said, "Great dinner, Sam. I didn't know you could cook."

"Yeah," chimed in Brittany.

Sam opened his mouth to speak when Josiah said, "Sam knows his way around the kitchen. Right, Sam?"

"Uh. . . Sure, Jos. Sure."

"It was great, Sam. Really great," said Brittany softly.

Feeling a little uncomfortable about the accolades, Sam's hands fumbled awkwardly with the adjustment to the DVR to start the movie as Josiah said, "Anyone want coffee? Or iced tea? Or a beer?"

Madison was the first to respond. "How about we start the movie first? I'd like to finish my dessert. But I'd sure like a beer after that."

"Me, too, Jos. After. . .," said Brittany.

Sam looked up from where he was adjusting the DVR and nodded agreement.

"OK," said Josiah, sinking into the sofa next to Madison. "Let's see what we were missing when we didn't see it first time around."

"Yeah," said Brittany.

The movie started and they all settled in to watch.

Christine Webb-Curtis and Dimity Hammon

Chapter 13 – Rehearsals

Joe assembled the cast and crew for the initial read-through of the play. After introductions, they all sat around a large table while each person read his or her part, only stopping when either they had a question or Joe had a comment. He encouraged them to be helpful to each other if they had observations that they thought useful. Rhys sat in a chair at the head of the table opposite Joe with one arm slung over the back and his body turned a little toward Dolores. He found her quite attractive and somehow familiar. But he had not been able to place her anywhere, so he let it go. He was very helpful and endearing to everyone, but gave particular attention to Dolores, praising her well-known acting skills.

He was surprised to see Marilyn at the table, but he was more interested in Dolores. He hoped Marilyn wasn't going to develop a crush on him, which would have been perfectly reasonable considering her situation. He didn't want to hurt her feelings, though, and it would make things uncomfortable during the play. Troy Douglas had secured a seat on his right and while Rhys wasn't sure about Marilyn, he sensed that, indeed, Troy had a crush on him. Oh well, it came with the territory, he figured.

They did two run-throughs and broke for the evening. All but Nico were committed to returning for rehearsal in the morning by eight thirty so they could get in a full day's worth of rehearsals. Nico said he would be able to join them in the afternoon again, barring unforeseen terrorist attacks or multiple murders. Joe told the actors that they had to be vigilant in learning their lines and expected that by tomorrow afternoon, they would be able to do their lines with only little reference to their scripts. In four days, they would be opening to a full house. Marilyn and Dolores walked out together chatting companionably.

¤ ¤ ¤

At the end of the afternoon, Lil and Nico arrived home at about the same time. As usual Nico prepared cocktails. He poured a gin and tonic for Lil, and a gin over ice with a twist of lemon peel for himself.

"I think I'll start dinner now, Cara. Why don't you relax with your book?"

"Good idea," Lil said putting her feet up on the chaise longue.

"Ooh. Sexy toes. . ."

"Well, thank you sir. I think so, too."

Nico stepped inside to start dinner while Lil reminded herself to tell him about the incident at the salon this morning. It never hurt for the local detective to know when there are marital problems in the neighborhood that could have serious consequences.

By the time he opened a bottle of Truro Vineyards 2010 pinot grigio, the sea bass and parsleyed lemon butter potatoes were done. He poured the wine, plated the fish and potatoes and called Lil in from the porch.

"Buon apetito, Cara," said Nico.

"Grazie e buon appetito a ti," said Lil.

Again they clinked glasses. Lil said, "lovely wine, Nico. And lovely dinner. Again grazie, mi Caro."

Nico leaned across for a buss.

"You noticed my pedicure earlier. It made me think that I wanted to tell you about the excitement that occurred at the salon."

"Oh?"

"A woman came in and accused one of the manicurists of having had an affair with her husband. It got a little ugly. The accused left. And the woman left looking to me as though she was feeling pretty victorious— actually a little like the cat that swallowed the canary."

"Who was it? D'you know her?"

"No, not exactly. But I've seen her before. Just can't place her. I didn't inquire. It would have been a little awkward, you know."

"I suppose. Well, I hope they work it out."

"Me, too. Wonderful fish, Nico. Again. . .," Lil smiled. "So rehearsals started today?"

"Yes they did. And by the way did you hear that Susan Dickenson's mother is very ill and she had to go to Maine, so she left the play?"

"Wow. So who took her place," asked Lil.

"Marilyn Horneby agreed to step in. She's always worked on the set but was happy to switch her roles for this production."

"Marilyn Horneby! She's the one, Nico."

"What one?"

"She's the one from the salon this afternoon."

"Oh. You mean the woman scorned?"

"Yeah. She's the one!"

"Well, let's hope it doesn't interfere with her acting."

"Yeah. Let's hope. . ." said Lil. "So Joe managed to complete the cast?"

"Not quite. We need someone to play one of the smaller but important parts—Mrs. White, and then two people for even smaller parts—the cook and the telegram deliverer."

"If you're having trouble with that, I can make a recommendation. Do you think Joe would be interested?"

"I don't think he'd turn anything down at this point. He's pretty desperate to fill those parts."

"There's a woman at St. Marks who has done some acting. I'm sure she could handle it. She dropped out of the theatre scene when her children were small."

"I think that'd be perfect. Maybe you could give her a call, and if she's willing, have her go to the theatre tomorrow. I'll call Joe and let him know.

¤ ¤ ¤

Lil met Mercedes Galvan when she first joined St. Marks. She was a valuable addition to the Social Responsibility Committee. They had become friends, and often talked about their "what if's" when they were preparing lunch for some Food Bank volunteers. Mercedes confided in Lil that she always wanted to do theatre but that she had a bad experience with an actor many years before, and she has since struggled to regain her confidence.

"Hello Meche. It's Lil."

"Hi. What's up?"

"Well, Nico and I were just talking about this summer's first playhouse production."

"And. . . .?"

"And it turns out that Joe Putnam's almost finished casting for his latest play and he needs someone for a small part. I thought you might be interested."

"Lil, you know how I feel about acting."

"Yes, I do. But I also know how much you miss it. And this part is a perfect way for you to ease back into it. Especially since it's a minor role."

"I don't know."

"Meche. How about looking at this as an opportunity for changing your life? And exactly what do you have to lose by taking this chance? Your self-confidence? The self-confidence that you lost all those many years ago?"

"Lil. . ."

"And what do you have to gain? Your confidence back? And many more years of joy in the theatre? Meche, I think you should seriously consider this. It'd be great for you. And I'd support you all the way. Rehearse with you if you want. Anything."

"Well. . ."

"I can tell him tonight if you want. Whaddya think?"

"I guess I can try. What's the worst that can happen?"

"You can forget your lines. . . Fall off the stage. . ."

"Thanks for the vote of confidence, Lil."

"Sure. Anytime," Lil kidded. "I'll let him know. And Mercedes, you'll be great."

"I hope so."

Christine Webb-Curtis and Dimity Hammon

Chapter 14 – Drinks and Dinner

As everyone was leaving the theatre after rehearsals that day, Rhys carefully and discreetly positioned himself near the door. Just as Dolores was heading to the exit, Rhys stepped out as if he were just preparing to exit and bumped into her.

"Oh, Dolores. So sorry. I simply wasn't paying enough attention."

Dolores, who didn't need any help in accidentally colliding with others, appeared to be just as sorry. "No, really Rhys. It's my fault. You know, I have to live up to my notorious reputation as clumsy. Anyway, no harm done."

"Absolutely, Dolores. And as long as neither of us can be sure who's at fault, could I suggest dinner? I have a table waiting at Lawson's. One more person wouldn't disappoint the wait staff, I'm sure."

"I don't know, Rhys. It's getting a little late. I really should eat in my room and work on my lines."

"Nonsense. I'm sure you've already got your lines down. And what better way to prepare than through the serenity of relaxation?"

"Well. I suppose I need to have dinner anyway."

"Excellent."

"But," said Dolores, "Let's not make a long evening of it, eh?"

"Certainly not. I, too, have to have some time to myself later this evening to rehearse. . . Of course, I suppose we could rehearse together." Rhys put his hand to his forehead as if to imply that he had just been thunderstruck by such a good idea.

"I'm not sure I'm ready for that yet. Do you mind if we talk about it tomorrow? Since we're both staying at Lawson's, we could maybe get together tomorrow night to rehearse. Would that work for you?"

"Absolutely. But since we both need to eat dinner, let's do that together also. And tomorrow we can plan on rehearsing after dinner. Yes?"

"I think that'll work."

"Brilliant, that's settled. So let's just go and have dinner now," Rhys said as they exited through the back door. "Look. There's my car. Can I give you a lift?"

"Oh, thanks, Rhys. I have a car. So I'll meet you there."

"You know, Dolores. If we return to the Inn together in my car, we can also drive back together in the morning. Then if you need your car tomorrow evening, you can pick it up tomorrow."

"No. I don't need to be going anywhere. I'll just leave the car here, then. Thanks. That makes sense. And very nice car, by the way. I'm in a rental—not so nice."

"Well thanks. I do love it. I've owned Jaguars my whole life. You know, you can take the man out of England but you can't take England out of the man."

"Clearly," said Dolores.

The drive to Lawson's took only five minutes as the theatre was located adjacent to the resort.

"My reservation is for seven. Why don't you join me then? I'll order you a drink. What do you drink?"

"Very kind. I'll have a glass of chardonnay," said Dolores. Thinking better of it, she said, "You know, on second thought, I'd like to wait until we're both seated. The chardonnay sounds good now, but I could easily change my mind by then. You know, life's too short to plan ahead."

"Too true, my dear. I'll see you, then, at seven."

¤ ¤ ¤

Rhys was already seated when Dolores appeared at the doorway to the restaurant looking very demure in her dimity print dress and thong sandals at the bottom of her glistening tanned legs. Around her shoulders was draped a delicately-woven bamboo scarf with a white and peach eucalyptus motif. Its softness invited touching. Rhys stood when she spotted him. On her wrist was a hand-hammered gold bangle, and her small earlobes were adorned with twisted gold hoops. She was accompanied to the table by the maitre d' who helped her to her seat.

"Evening, Dolores. You DO look a vision."

"Well, thank you, Rhys. As do you."

"Does mademoiselle care for a cocktail? Aperitif?"

"Yes, thank you. I think I'd like a Kir."

"Very nice. And you, sir? Another martini?"

"Yes, please. That would be lovely?"

Off he went to fetch their drinks while Rhys remarked on the evening view toward the sea. "This is a wonderful place to be enjoying a meal together. Don't you think?"

"Absolutely. And thanks for the invitation, Rhys. Even when we work together, sometimes it's hard to get to know each other without going the extra mile."

"I agree. Of course, this theatre venue is much more relaxed than New York, don't you think?"

"True. I don't do a lot of theatre these days."

"That's the appeal of Joe's plays. We all need a live production to keep our skills up. And I love coming to the Cape. I even have family here, which gives me a good excuse to commit myself to a summer play occasionally."

"Really? That's nice. Tell me about them."

"Why don't we take a look at the menu first? And perhaps you'd like a starter?"

"I think I would. Yes."

"I see there are some Nobscusset oysters. I believe that's local to Yarmouth here on Cape Cod. Would you like to try those?"

"I'm not really an oyster fan. But I'd like to try the tuna tartare."

"All right," said Rhys signaling to the waiter.

"Yes, sir. And would you like a wine with that?"

"Certainly. What do you suggest, then? Something of the best quality, of course."

"Of course, Sir. Perhaps the Spy Valley Sauvignon Blanc?"

"That would be fine, then. We'll order dinner shortly."

"Very well, Sir."

"Now where were we? Oh yes, you were going to tell me about your family here on Cape Cod."

"Oh yes," said Rhys, pointing toward the window. "I have a niece who lives on the Cape. Look, Dolores. The sun is beginning to color the sky. There."

"Very nice. Very dramatic and fitting for such a dinner, don't you think?"

"Absolutely. So, Dolores. Where do you hail from? You seem a little mysterious to me."

"Do I?" Dolores smiled as much to herself as to Rhys for having been able to project such a reaction. "I haven't meant to give that impression. Perhaps it's just that initial shyness."

"Shy? You? How's that possible? You must have had vast experience in social and professional situations."

"I'm an actress, Rhys. I act."

After their dinner, Dolores appeared to be ready to leave when Rhys called the waiter over.

"Yes, Sir."

"We'd like a cognac, please. The Léopold Gourmel."

"Yes sir. Right away."

"Rhys, I'm really beginning to tire. Perhaps tomorrow?"

"I agree that tomorrow would be ideal to have a cognac to get us started in our readings. But really, Dolores, I can't allow you to leave the table without enjoying a Gourmel. I assure you, you won't be disappointed."

Dolores was itching to return to her room to think through her strategy. Though Rhys' interest in her was going according to plan, she knew she had to be careful.

"All right, then. Just one glass. Then I'm off until the morning, Rhys."

"Of course, my dear. Of course."

Christine Webb-Curtis and Dimity Hammon

Chapter 15 – Suspicion

Nico arrived home to find Lil in the kitchen making her famous tamale pie--one of his favorites.

"What's the occasion, Cara?"

"Just had a hankering for something a little more plebian, if you don't mind. And tamale pie seemed just the right thing."

"Works for me. I love it. How about I make us some margaritas in honor of the southwestern theme?"

"Well, I'd certainly appreciate that, m'dear. And how'd your rehearsal go?"

"Truthfully, watching these actors interact was theatre on its own."

Nico finished preparing the margaritas for both of them. Lil raised her glass to take a sip while he said, "Each actor is so attuned to his role in the production—separate from each other actor. It's almost as if the concept of team was unfamiliar to any of them."

"Even Meche and that other person— the woman whose husband was running around?"

"No, no. Not the amateur actors. It's the career actors who are pouty like little children. All except Eric Shiller, not surprisingly. He seems to be oblivious to all the tension, all the drama. I think more than anyone I've ever known, he is mighty happy to be in his skin."

"Good for him. He deserves it—what with all he and his family have suffered already. So tell me more," said Lil as she put her tamale pie in the oven.

"Yes. Well, now that you can sit down for a bit, I'll give you the blow by blow."

"Goodie," Lil said, rubbing her hands together and again showing her impish grin.

"Don't leave anything out, Nico. I wanna hear everything."

"I'll try not to disappoint, Cara," said Nico, leaning in as if he didn't want to be overheard—even in his own house.

He began, "So we all sat around the table. Joe was at one end and Rhys at the other. Dolores Darrington sat next to Rhys. She's playing Miss Scarlet, by the way. And Troy Douglas sat on his other side."

"He's the butler, right?"

"Right. And then Eric was at the other end of the table to Joe's left. I was in the middle between Darrington and Meche. Then on the other side of Meche was Bertha—next to Joe. And across from me was Marilyn Horneby."

166

"Ah, yes. She's the one from the salon. Our woman with the wandering husband, eh?"

"Yup. And then Ted Dickenson. Remember his wife had to leave town because of her ailing mother, and the Horneby woman took her role. But Ted is playing Mr. Boddy."

"Can't actually remember that character, but never mind. Tell me about the process. What was it like?"

"So. We ran through the play line by line. But it was the more subtle interaction that I noticed at the end of the table. I could swear Troy Douglas was trying way too hard to get the attention of Rhys Traynor. Also I'm sure--without a doubt--that Traynor was trying to attract the attention of Dolores Darrington."

"Very funny, Nico. But do you think that Rhys Traynor is gay?"

"No. I really don't. But maybe Douglas thinks he might be. Or that he might be able to persuade him to see the error of his ways—so to speak."

"Hmmm. Never occurred to me. So what about the rest of the people at the table?"

"I sense that Marilyn Horneby has some attraction toward Traynor. On the other hand, I thought Ms. Drama Queen,

Bertha Poppe, displayed some hostility toward the man. I have no idea what that was about. But it was just an intuition."

"Your intuition is pretty keen, Nico."

"The other thing about Traynor is that he seems to be distracted unrelated to the play.

"Because. . .?"

"He must have popped out to take a call a half dozen times just while I was there. And he fidgeted with his phone in a way that made me think he was worried about what the caller might say and he wanted to get it over with."

"I imagine that might have been pretty annoying to all the others—especially Joe."

"I'm sure it was. He claimed he was negotiating a role and that the negotiations were at a delicate stage."

"Hmmm. Sounds like you're thinking it's something else, eh? Look, I've gotta finish dinner. Why don't you enjoy the porch while I pull the rest of dinner together. We're going to eat out there anyway."

"Sure. I'll wander on out there and maybe run through my lines again."

"And maybe you can tell me more when we're having dinner."

"Oh, believe me, there's more to tell. Anything I can do to help?"

"Sure. But not tonight. You go relax. I'll join you soon."

Nico leaned in to plant a smooch on his wife's forehead and headed out to the porch.

¤ ¤ ¤

The girls were delighted to run into Nico and Lil the next day at Trader Joe's in Hyannis. They hadn't seen them since Joe and Annie's wedding, and all of them were eager to catch up. Lil had developed a real fondness for both girls, but especially Madison who seemed so like her own daughter. They were both independent and feisty—and bright besides. It was crowded and busy in the store so they decided to go next door to the White Whale Cafe instead. The girls were happy to find out that Nico and Lil had decided to stay on the Cape for good.

Over cappuccinos, they caught up on goings on since they last saw each other. After they were all updated, Nico turned the conversation to present-day interests. "So girls, have you come across any mysteries that you need some backup for?"

Nico knew all too well that the girls thought that they had almost single handedly solved the mystery of the dead porn star on

169

the beach the year before and that he had only provided some assistance.

"Well, now that you mention it. . ." Brittany began.

"There is something funny going on next door to our cottage," finished Madison.

"Really," Lil's eyebrows shot up--always interested in a potential mystery.

"The place looks deserted, but the other day these guys arrived in a big fancy speedboat and they went into that house."

"Yeah," added Madison. "Our place is on that little bay that empties out completely at low tide--Onion Bay--and you never see boats there. It's too risky. But these guys just roared up on shore. Of course they got stuck."

"Nico, you know where they are," said Lil. "Remember we went clamming there with the Dickensons during the low tides in the winter."

"Of course I remember. Those clams were great! But I can't imagine anyone trying to bring a big boat in there."

"And that's not all," interrupted Madison. "We had to go over there to get Dixie. . ."

"Wait a minute, who's Dixie?"

"Brit's cat, and anyway, those guys were really nervous and said they were lost and they had to get out of there, but they didn't! They went back into the house. So, when it got dark we went over there, but we couldn't see anything."

"You what," barked Nico, leaning forward with a pained look on his face. "Tell me you didn't go over there while those guys were there, please!"

"Oh we know what we're doing. No one would ever see us and besides we had Josiah and Sam with us."

"Oh that makes me feel so much better," Nico said sarcastically. "They're the perfect body guards, for sure."

"Anyway, we knew they were in the house 'cause the boat was still there, but the shades were all down and we couldn't see a thing. They were still there when we got back to our cottage, but the boat was gone in the morning. Don'cha think that sounds fishy?"

"Yes it does," Nico replied. "I'll look into it."

"Oh you don't need to worry," said Brittany. "We've got it covered. We'll let you know if anything comes of it."

"Yes, well sure. But in the meantime is there anything else that struck you as funny over there? Any little thing that might help us, um, you know, figure out what's going on?"

"Oh I remember another thing," Madison scowled. "Brit, remember we saw that car there, too?"

"My, my," said Lil. "The plot thickens! Anyway Nico, we need to get on our way. So nice to see you again girls and I'm sure it won't be the last time this summer! It'd be nice to see you at dinner on Sunday. If not this Sunday, then another one."

"That'd be great, Mizz Forgione," said Madison.

"'Lil,' Madison."

"Sorry. 'Lil.'"

"This Sunday'd be great, then," said Brittany. "But we'd better check our schedule at Lawson's before we really commit."

"Sure. Good idea," said Lil.

"We'll let you know tomorrow," said Madison, "if that works."

"That'll be fine. You take care then."

"And that means," said Nico sternly, "that you should stay away from your neighbor's house for the time being."

"Well. . .," said Madison. "We'll try. But no promises."

Chapter 16 – Preparations

Marilyn watched Traynor limp his way to the stage with his cell phone plastered to the side of his head. He spoke into the phone, his face contorted in what looked like real pain. He shut the phone and shoved it into his pocket as he arrived at the bottom of the few short steps that went up to the stage. He seemed to struggle some with his cane and leg as he made his way onto the stage and sat dramatically in his usual chair at the end of the table.

Marilyn had changed her daily walking routine from morning to night to help her with the stress of the past few weeks. She found that she desperately needed the release of tension at the end of the day rather than at the beginning. What with her husband's philandering and the feelings associated with that, she was struggling with her commitment to the play. She questioned her willingness to take over for Susan Dickenson. At the time she thought it would distract her. Instead, it kept that misery close. In addition Marilyn found herself spending a lot of time--too much really--thinking about Rhys, imagining being with him again, what it would be like. She felt like a silly schoolgirl. The evening walks were a godsend and made it possible for her to actually sleep at night.

Two nights ago, Marilyn was passing Onion Bay and saw a car backing up to the garage of the dark unrented cottage. She was struck by the incongruity of it and walked closer to the car and house. No one seemed to be around so she crept to the edge of the sand dune at the rear of the cottages where she hunkered down. When her eyes became accustomed to the quickly disappearing dusk, she saw movement at the rear of the cottage. The garage door opened and a burly man ducked out, pushing it up in the process. He emerged from the garage and walked to the car carrying a package, which he put into the open trunk. Returning to the garage, he closed the door as the car moved off down the road.

When she looked back at the cottage, the garage door was shut and it again looked deserted. She then noticed an old Volvo in the driveway of the house next door. Towels hung all over the porch and empties spilled out of the garbage can. She figured that was some young person's summer digs.

¤ ¤ ¤

Traynor seemed to spend a lot of time making and taking cell phone calls. At least three times during every rehearsal he would leave the set abruptly to answer a call. A few times he never came back and his car would be gone when the rehearsal was finished. Marilyn was surprised that a pro like Joe Putnam would put up with such nonsense.

When he was an hour late for rehearsal that morning throwing everyone else off schedule, Joe asked him if he could try to be on time from now on. Traynor again apologized profusely saying he was so sorry to mess up this great production.

Putnam sighed and said "I hope so."

Again, Rhys apologized for his tardiness, explaining that he was at a delicate stage in negotiations for his next role.

Joe shrugged his shoulders and continued. "Can we do a clean walk-through at the table and see if we can get to the stage by today. We open the day after tomorrow— dress rehearsal tomorrow--and we've got a lot of ground to cover. And please, people. We've got to work through today. Any questions?"

"Yes, Joe," said Rhys.

"Rhys. Something else?"

"I'm so sorry but I have an obligation this afternoon. I might be a bit late for rehearsal."

"I would very much appreciate it if you could change the time of your other obligation to keep your commitment to your obligation here."

"I'll make every effort to show up on time, Joe."

Trying to hold his temper, Joe said, "Let's get to work, people. Clearly we'd better make the best of the entire cast while we can." He shot a look at Rhys. "From the beginning, then. . ."

Nico looked around at the full effects of the discomfort on the rest of the cast resulting from Joe and Traynor's exchange. He noticed Dolores looking smug, Troy looking perturbed, Eric and Meche looking anywhere but at another person, and Marilyn appearing—if his instincts were right—as if, like Nico, she were assessing the impact of the conversation on the rest of the players.

¤ ¤ ¤

On the way to their respective cars late in the afternoon, Rhys and Dolores waved at each other flirtatiously and made the short drive up to Lawson's. At seven p.m., Dolores entered the dining room once again to find Rhys seated at his table overlooking the golf course and having what appeared to be a heated conversation on his cell phone. His hand was cupped over the area between the phone and his mouth in an effort to make sure no one else could hear the conversation. Though his mouth was not visible, the furrow between his eyes made it clear that the topic was not all milk and honey. When he saw Dolores, he immediately held up his hand in a short wave and seemed to rush the caller off the phone. He stood up awkwardly to make up for the delay in his greeting and the chair crashed to the floor. The maître d' picked it up immediately and restored it to its proper place.

"Sorry for my clumsiness," said Rhys to Dolores rather than to the maître d' who had rescued the chair.

"Well. Wasn't that quite the welcome?" said Dolores while the maître d' helped her to get settled. At least it wasn't my clumsiness this time."

"You're not the only one who might appear occasionally inelegant, my dear. Would you like an aperitif or a drink?"

"Yes, please. I'd like a very dry martini, if you please, sir," she said looking at the maître d'. "And you might let the waiter know that we'd like to order soon as we have some work to do this evening."

"Certainly, Madam. I'd be glad to. And you, Sir?"

"I'll have the same, thank you."

The maître d' left the table for the drinks as Rhys and Dolores pored over their menus in anticipation of the prompt appearance of their waiter who arrived to serve drinks. He recited the evening specials and took their dinner orders, leaving them to enjoy their martinis.

By eight fifteen, they were meandering toward Rhys' room with their scripts. As they entered, Rhys spread his arm to the expanse of the sitting area of the suite and said, "Would you like to work here, my dear? Or would you prefer the deck?"

"The deck sounds good to me," she said, thinking it would be fine if there were witnesses—just in case Rhys got the better of her.

"And can I offer you something to drink?"

"Thank you, Rhys. Maybe in a bit. In the meantime, I brought some water. Shall we get started?"

"Sure. No problem," said Rhys, wondering how he would entice this woman into his arms.

"Maybe we could start at page seven. I'll read the women and asides and you read the men. OK?"

"OK."

"And we can skip the fanny squeeze that precedes the dialogue."

"Awww. That's the best part," said Rhys feigning disappointment—or rather feigning the feigning of disappointment. . .

The two continued their reading for an hour and Dolores said, "Perhaps it's time for that drink."

"Perfect. What can I get for you?"

"Do you have the cognac that we enjoyed last night at dinner? The Léopold Gourmel?"

"I think I do. Please. Sit down here while I get it."

"Oh, no. I'm happy to wait on you, Rhys. After all, you've been so gracious," said Dolores delighted with her opportunity.

"Very kind, Dolly," said Rhys. "May I call you 'Dolly'?"

"Dolly. Hmmm. No one's ever called me that. So why not? As long as it's not Lollie. And Dolly'll be just between us."

"Brilliant, then. And why don't we move inside for our drinks? The mosquitos are beginning to get to me."

They moved through the screen door to the sitting area. Dolores went to the bar and took glasses from the shelf. She opened the bottle of cognac and poured each a glass. "Here you are, Rhys," said Dolores, swirling their glasses. "Let's drink to a good run with Clue."

"Cin, cin," said Rhys, swirling his cognac as well and touching Dolores' glass with his.

◻ ◻ ◻

Jim Horneby was in trouble. He knew he had really screwed up with Marilyn and in the process embarrassed himself with the entire town. He had to go on an extended business trip to avoid facing anyone. In addition, Thuan walked out on him so he had no playmates at the moment. To make matters worse, his extra job delivering packages around New England was in jeopardy. Though he was aware that the packages he was delivering were probably contraband or, even more serious, drugs, it was easy for him to combine sales calls with the deliveries. Like most petty criminals, he never considered that he would get caught and the money was quick and plentiful. He didn't do any deliveries on the Cape, however, because it was someone else's territory. He picked up the parcels from some guys in a sleek speed boat in a little bay near the channel that separated the Cape from the mainland and dropped them off at various places around his sales territory. His orders came through anonymous cell phone calls with very short notice. He sensed that if he refused to make a pick-up and drop, the consequences would be unpleasant.

He found it strange when he saw the same speed boat go into Onion Bay near his house. He had slipped into his home to get a few things when Marilyn was rehearsing at the playhouse.

'That must be where those guys deliver to their agent here on the Cape,' he thought. Curious, he drove over to the edge of the Bay just in time to see the boat pull up in front of a deserted cottage. He waited for a moment and then saw an old red Toyota Corolla pull up by the garage. His interest piqued, he watched his own contact put a bag in the trunk just as he did with Jim. And the driver then flew back down that road as if he might have become infected by the contact. Jim thought he recognized the driver but wasn't absolutely sure because of the wool cap pulled down low over his forehead.

'Aha,' thought Jim. 'This looks like an opportunity for a little more money on the side here, if I'm right. I think I'll pay a visit to him tomorrow. He has a reputation to keep and probably running drugs wouldn't improve that reputation.'

Christine Webb-Curtis and Dimity Hammon

Chapter 17 – Couples

Sam's cabinet making mentor, Mr. Tashima, was renowned for his expertise in fine cabinetry. He had been consulted on the compilation of the new Duncan Phyfe exhibit at the Metropolitan Museum of Art in New York and suggested that Sam visit the exhibit to see how fine cabinetry was produced in the eighteenth and nineteenth centuries. The exhibit had opened the previous week to an enthusiastic reception in the press. Mr. Tashima figured it would be inspirational to Sam and encouraged him to check it out. Sam had never been to New York, but Friday was his next day off, and he planned to ask Brittany if she would go with him to New York—and take her car. He wanted to spend the day with her at least, and besides, his own car might not make it.

When Madison and Brittany were on their way back to Lawson's on Thursday for their duty on the lunch staff, Brittany told Madison about Sam's having asked her to go on Friday.

"Friday?" said Madison. "That's tomorrow."

"Oh," she mused. "I guess it is. He only asked me yesterday and I forgot to tell you. Ms. Butler said it'd be OK as long as you were around to take care of the lunch crowd."

"Thanks a lot, Brit," said Madison—her voice tinged with sarcasm.

"Sorry I didn't tell you sooner—or maybe even ask you. But you get to keep the extra tips. That's nice."

"I guess. So you're going all the way to New York and back tomorrow? How long'll that take?"

"Sam said it's a four and a half-hour drive. If we leave at five thirty, we'd get there at ten. We could do the museum, have lunch someplace, maybe even have dinner there, too, then drive back."

"That's nine hours of driving, Brit. Are you nuts?"

"No. Sam'll do at least half the driving. It'll be fine. I've only been to New York with my parents. It'll be a real adventure."

"It'll be that, then. Let's just hope the lunch crowd isn't overwhelming."

"I'll owe you one, Maddy."

¤ ¤ ¤

At the end of the afternoon, Josiah saw Madison walking toward the parking lot and shouted after her. "Madison. Wait up."

"Hey, Josiah. What's goin' on?"

"Since Sam and Brittany are running off to the Big Apple, I was thinking that maybe you and I could do something tomorrow after work. I've wanted to eat at the Quirky Quahog in Bourne but never got it together. Interested?"

"Yeah. Sure. Great idea. Except for crossing the bridge to get here, I've never been to Bourne, so you can show me around."

"Well, I don't know that much about what's to see in Bourne, but after we eat, we can go over to the Canal and watch the boat traffic. It's pretty neat."

"I'm willing. So we'll go after work, then. Do you wanna meet here at the Inn or what?"

"I don't mind picking you up at the cottage."

"To tell the truth, I wasn't sure how I was gonna get back to the cottage since Brittany's gone with her car, so I'll meet you here and then you can take me back after dinner. OK? Anyway, I'll probably have to take a taxi just to get here in the morning."

"Hey. I'll pick you up tomorrow morning on my way in."

"It's way out of your way, isn't it?"

"So what. It's no problem."

"That'd be great. Thanks."

¤ ¤ ¤

Now that she had found a way to get in and out without being trapped, Dixie liked it in the garage of the deserted house next door. Because it was unoccupied for so long, there were lots of mice—as well as soft old clothes and rugs for her to sleep on. There were also fun toys--pieces of wire and chunks of forgotten steel wool. One that she particularly liked was dropped by that guy that sometimes came in and out and talked to her. She'd heard it drop on the concrete floor when the guy was rummaging around. He looked for it with his flashlight but gave up in frustration. Dixie saw where it dropped and went over to investigate as soon as he left the garage. It looked a bit like the sort of thing Brittany wore around her neck. It was shiny and long with something else bigger and shiny at the end. She liked grabbing one end in her mouth and dragging it around the floor. It made a neat sound. Then when she tossed it in the air with her claw, the big part would twist around and around. It was a little like a snake that didn't try to get away. When she held the bigger part in her teeth and pawed at it for a while, it popped open to reveal another shiny thing that sprang up. And when she let go, it went back inside. The thing that came out looked a lot like what Brittany used to scoop out her food from the cat food can. Another thing had popped up that looked like what Brittany drank her milk out of, only much smaller. All told, Dixie liked this new toy enough to hide it under her favorite sleeping place to play with later.

Despite their best intentions Brittany and Sam didn't get on the road to New York until six thirty. They both thought it was an ungodly hour anyway so they were quite smug about it. Brittany had given up on keeping Dixie inside. She usually returned at some point in the wee hours for no apparent reason other than to see if Brittany was still alive and able to feed her before she left for work. On that morning, however, Dixie was nowhere to be found when Brittany got up at five. Trying to be quiet so she wouldn't wake up Madison, Brittany went outside to find the cat. Dixie usually spent the day sleeping on Brittany's bed, which made her think the cat was safe. She walked around the cottage calling softly and spotted her over by the deserted house next door. Dixie looked up when she heard her name, but went right back to playing with something. Brittany swore under her breath, knowing that now she would be late picking up Sam and walked over to get the cat. She saw that Dixie's toy was a necklace of some sort. She bent down for a closer look while Dixie sat back, hoping that Brittany would appreciate the present she found and maybe give her a few more treats. She turned the necklace over and saw that it was a nice silver locket on a chain. As Brittany pulled on the chain, Dixie stretched over it with her paw and the locket sprang open revealing a tiny cup and spoon inside.

"Wow, Dixie," whispered Brittany. "This is way cool! Good find!"

Brittany closed the locket and absent-mindedly put it on, then picked up the cat, hurrying back into the cottage to get ready to leave. She fed Dixie and included a couple of extra treats before she headed out.

Sam was waiting when Brittany pulled into his driveway, but he, too, had been a bit late getting ready.

"This is going to be great, Brit," Sam said enthusiastically as he got in.

"You bet. I haven't been to New York for years. The last time I was with my Mom and Dad, which was fun, but you know. . ."

"Well first time for me and I can't wait to see the exhibit. I want to see everything really--Central Park, the Empire State Building, all of it!"

"I don't think we can see it all and still get back in time to go to work tomorrow, but who knows? It'll be good!"

They headed to Providence and then south on Route 95 through places Sam had never been before—Warwick, Groton, Bridgeport, and over the Robert Kennedy Bridge onto Manhattan Island. They made good time even though they hit some rush hour traffic. They were taken aback by the cost of parking at the museum, but having little choice, they left the car there for the day so they could explore once they finished with the exhibit.

Sam was awestruck with the craftsmanship of Duncan Phyfe. He could not imagine ever developing enough skill to replicate such pieces and felt a newfound motivation to work even harder with his mentor. He was very grateful for Mr. Tashima's suggestion that he should see the exhibit. Brittany visited the Fabergé exhibit and the collection of American Indian Art while Sam took his time to carefully study the cabinetry details. They met at the entrance as planned. They were tempted to have lunch there at the museum, but decided instead to wander down Fifth Avenue toward Rockefeller Center to find a deli.

After lunch they strolled over to Times Square on the off chance that they could get tickets to a matinee. As luck would have it, they were able to grab tickets for amazingly good seats at the hit Broadway musical, "The Book of Mormon," which left them breathless.

They had dinner at a perfect little bistro on Eighth Avenue. The whole day had been impossibly romantic, and they held hands as they walked up Central Park West. It only seemed natural to pause for a kiss or two as they crossed the park back to the car, and the mood stayed with them as they took turns driving back to the Cape.

¤ ¤ ¤

Madison emerged from the back of the Inn just as Josiah arrived at his car in the staff parking lot. He stood at the door of his car looking back toward the eighteenth green and the back of the Inn as Madison appeared around the corner waving. Josiah waved back and walked to the back of the car to greet her.

"Ready to go?" asked Josiah.

"Hell yeah. Soooo ready."

"Let's then."

After dinner, Josiah and Madison headed to the canal to watch the boats pass through. They parked on the edge of the canal and sat on the front of Josiah's car with his bleacher cushions.

"Nice dinner, eh?" asked Josiah.

"Very. I'll have to admit I like it lots better when I'm not the one serving."

Josiah smiled and patted her on the arm. "Yeah. I get it."

"Y'know, Jos. The whole year at school, we never once did anything like this."

"I know. Seems strange, doesn't it? It just seems kinda comfortable."

"Yea. That's what I was thinking, too."

Turning her attention toward the canal, she said, "Where are these boats going—all along the canal anyway?"

"Well, they're either going to the north side of the Cape or the south side. Or they're going farther—up to Boston or down to Rhode Island and more. The Maritime Academy is across the way over there," he said pointing. "When I was a kid, I fantasized about going there, but my Mum was way smarter than I was about it. She's the one who suggested Bowdoin."

"Well I'm glad she did," Madison said throwing him a flirty look. "Yikes. Some of these boats are enormous. Look at that one!"

"An ocean liner. Hmmm. Doesn't appeal to me. I can't imagine paying lots of money to ride from port to port in a hotel. It just doesn't make sense."

"I suppose. But there's something very romantic about it, don'tcha think?"

"Maybe."

"Hey. Look at that! That's the boat from next door. See?"

"Well, maybe." He looked a little more closely. "I think you're right. Or at least that big guy there looks like the one you described."

"Wonder where they're going."

"Dunno. But they seem in a pretty big hurry. If they don't slow down, they're gonna get cited for speeding."

"Really? That happens?"

"You bet it does."

"Y'know, Jos. I'm getting a little mosquito·y. D'ya think we could go back to the cottage?"

"Sure. Let's."

It was after two in the morning when Sam and Brittany got to his place and were happy to see that Josiah's car was not there.

"He and Madison went out tonight," said Brittany. "Do you think. . . ?"

"Yes I do and, ah, it would probably be really rude for you to, like. . ."

"Yeah, maybe. . ."

The next morning Brittany and Madison managed to make it in to work on

time as did Sam and Josiah--all of them a
little more cheerful than usual.

Christine Webb-Curtis and Dimity Hammon

Chapter 18 – Opening Night

Casey had enjoyed a most entertaining time the previous night. Not only had he encountered one of those striped cats that smelled so good and always got such a fun reaction from his human, but he found a rubber bag toy filled with white stuff when he was chasing that tabby cat at the house down the road. He threw it around for a while at the cottage and decided to take it home where he could finish it off in his own time. Unfortunately, his human was up early complaining about how much Casey stunk and took the toy back into the house. Casey had to stay tied up in the washtub for quite a while in some fizzy stuff that was sprayed on him. When he was finally rinsed off and allowed back into the house from his garage purgatory, his toy was nowhere to be found.

Ted was puzzled when he found the bag in his front yard, but he was too busy to pay attention to it when he realized that, once again, Casey had been chasing a skunk. He put the bag on the kitchen counter while he washed Casey in the peroxide, baking soda, shampoo mixture he kept on hand for just such an emergency. He finished rinsing the dog, who was used to this and as good natured as always. Then he locked him in the garage to dry off. As he passed the kitchen counter, he noticed the bag and decided it was suspicious enough to take to Nico's on Monday when he was having dinner with them.

¤ ¤ ¤

The play opened to an enthusiastic review from the local newspaper despite the backstage anguish. After all, one advantage to Clue is that no one is exactly sure how it's going to turn out, which provides a little cushion for the occasional miscues. The professional actors did very well on stage as expected. And the amateur actors did well, too, considering they all thought they would drag the production down with their inexperience. Joe was pleased with the play and expressed his thanks effusively to all with a reception backstage—catered by his wife, of course, and offering champagne and delectable treats for them all.

Nico was feeling mighty satisfied about having actually remembered his few lines and made it through the performance without embarrassing himself. After all, it'd be bad if Falmouth's Chief Detective acted like a buffoon.

Lil had joined them back stage and seemed to enjoy the ambiance. "I'm going over to talk to Meche. She seems a bit lost," said Lil.

"OK, Cara. I'd like to try another one of those oysters if I can get to them before they're gone."

Nico found his way to the table only to find the oysters had disappeared, and he had to settle on a stuffed mushroom instead. Also delicious, he found.

He glanced over to see Rhys fixed on something or someone. Nico moved a little away from the table and could see that Marilyn Horneby and Dorothy Darrington appeared to be deep in conversation a few steps away from the crowd.

'Interesting,' Nico thought. 'And there he is back on the phone again. I don't get this cell phone obsession, but I guess it goes with the territory.'

¤ ¤ ¤

Eric and his family were enjoying their cottage. Both Parker, their second child, and Sara, the older of the two, were even-tempered and happy most of the time, which made travel with them virtually trouble free.

The Shillers weren't accustomed to such luxury and found themselves alternately awestruck and delighted. Jennie was able to take the children to the beach after dropping Eric off at the theatre for rehearsals. She would return to the cottage for the children's lunch and naps and go back to the theatre for

Eric. Then she would either sit in the audience or wait back stage in the dressing room area depending on how calm the children were. She felt it was a wonderful opportunity for the kids—travel, theatre, the ocean. And Sara was a delightfully social child, easily making friends with most of both cast and crew. Unlike the rest of them, however, neither Rhys nor Troy was inclined to cozy up to small children. Too young for flirtation in the case of Rhys and utterly mystifying to Troy. He never wanted them, never spent time around them, never appreciated them, didn't pay attention to them. He was a regular curmudgeon when it came to anyone under twelve.

Eric was exhibiting his natural positive attitude and enthusiasm. Despite his experience with Joe's former girlfriend, Celine, who had treated him very badly, he maintained a strong sense of optimism and trust in others that grew out of his Midwestern naïveté. He appreciated his good luck at being on Cape Cod in the first place, and he planned to gain as much experience as he could—both from the more experienced stage actors and from Joe whose stage direction, he presumed, would be quite different from his movie direction. He was childishly excited by the whole venture and seemed innately unable to find anything untoward about it. On the second day of rehearsals he felt confident enough to take a deep breath and watch the real pros go to work.

Eric's wife, Jennie, and their daughter, Sara, were in the audience for the first evening's production. Lawson's was more than happy to offer up a babysitter free of charge for Jennie—considered by all one of the nicest guests staff had had the pleasure of serving. Her midwestern demeanor was a welcome change from the likes of Rhys Traynor and the rest of the professionals staying at Lawson's and who treated staff as if they were there for the sole purpose of serving only them. Besides, the children were charming—especially Sara whose social skills outpaced her chronological age. And Parker was easy to entertain. Brittany and Madison's boss, Ms. Butler, asked her niece, Meaghan, if she would be willing to take care of Parker, and she was more than happy to do it. She had an arrangement with the assistant manager that she would be paid later and not to accept any money from Eric or Jennie. After feeding the baby his dinner, she walked over to the main lodge and watched over him while he entertained the guests sitting in the main room enjoying their papers, writing their letters and talking. Parker was having a glorious evening. And

Meaghan enjoyed the attention she got just from watching over this funny little boy.

Jennie and Sara sat in the third row on the end to make sure Sara could see her daddy at his best on stage. At the end of the production, they went back stage to join in the festivities. Sara passed among all but Rhys and Troy whom she had known from her prior encounters as cold and grouchy. Jennie stood back quietly letting Eric and Sara get all the attention. She was quite content with her spot on the edge of the scene.

Out of the corner of her eye, Jennie noticed Rhys and Bertha near the stage door with their heads bent together, exchanging what appeared to be uncomfortable words. Bertha lifted her finger toward Rhys' chest and stabbed at it a few times. He swiped her hand away and she stumbled back, turned and pushed the door open so hard, it flew against the wall, and out she stomped. Just as Rhys looked back at Jennie, she turned her attention back to the others as quickly as she could. Red-faced, she could hardly contain herself, knowing that she had not intended to pry. She was raised to stay out of other people's business and she felt nothing but embarrassment over the incident.

Rhys walked toward her just as Joe sidled up and put his arm around her shoulder.

"Well, Jennie. How'd you feel about the evening?"

Stammering a little, Jennie was grateful for the distraction. "Oh, Mr. Putnam. I thought it was special. I laughed and gasped along with everyone else in the audience. The whole thing was great."

"Please, Jennie. Call me 'Joe.'"

Jennie looked down and back up smiling sweetly. Hesitantly, she said, "Sure. Joe. OK."

"And Sara? She seems to be in her element here, doesn't she?"

"Well frankly, any element full of friendly people is her element, Joe."

"Yes. She's quite the little butterfly. And very precocious. Anytime you think you might like to have her do any acting, please let me know."

"Oh," she said as her hand moved up to her chest. "I never thought about it. That'd be something, wouldn't it? Thanks for that. I don't know if that's what we want Sara to be doing with her life. We'd have to really think about it. But I appreciate your saying such nice things about her. She certainly is a joy."

"No question. We feel the same way about our Sophie as well."

"You should. She's lovely."

"Thanks, Jennie. Well, enjoy the rest of the evening."

"Thanks, Joe."

¤ ¤ ¤

At the end of the evening, Joe addressed the cast and crew. "I'd like to thank you all for having done such a great job. It looks as though we'll have a good run. I hope you've enjoyed the evening. Now go home and get some rest. And I'll see you here tomorrow at noon for the matinee at two.

"Well then, ladies and gentlemen," announced Rhys in his best thespian voice. "I will take my leave. It has been a pleasure working with you all. And I look forward to tomorrow afternoon. But I am heading back for a good night's rest and will see you all on the 'morrow."

"G'night, Rhys," echoed back from the crowd.

As Rhys went to his car, Marilyn bid her goodbyes as well and left right behind him. She had doubts about his returning to Lawson's for the night. She was truly smitten and wanted to know where he was going; but she was spent after her first night on the stage and thought better of chasing him around instead of taking care of herself.

¤ ¤ ¤

"What a great time, Nico," said Lil as he escorted her out the door.

"I agree—wholeheartedly."

Approaching their car, Nico watched one of the actors drive off with somewhat more haste than seemed necessary. As he got into the car, he made a call to Sergeant Kellerman who had just left with his partner, Marc. They had been Nico's guests at the after party. Nico kept thinking about the story the girls had told him about the cottage next to theirs. He asked Kellerman to drive by the girls' cottage before he signed off for the night. He had a feeling there was something wrong, but he couldn't quite figure out what it was or who was involved.

"What was that about, Nico?"

"Oh, I dunno. Just playing it safe. I'm sure it's nothing, Cara."

"Didn't sound like 'nothing' to me!"

"Aww. Let's go home and enjoy a limoncello before we turn in. Whaddya say, eh?"

"Perfect way to avoid the questions. But in your own time. And anyway, I'd love

203

that. Let's. And it's a perfect night to have it on the porch."

"It's a date, then."

¤ ¤ ¤

The old Toyota tore out of the remote parking lot as the driver cursed under his breath at his predicament. Here he was again having to do the bidding of those idiots. And why did they make me drive this awful little car? Clutching the steering wheel, white knuckled, he was barely able to focus on the road ahead and almost missed the turn to Onion Bay—or whatever it was called.

¤ ¤ ¤

Marilyn was passing Onion Bay on her way home and decided to park there and take her evening walk. Though she was tired, she thought a walk might do her good. She knew these woods and paths well--even in the dark. She parked her car and found her way to the dune behind the two cottages. After she had seen the Volvo in the theatre parking lot, she realized that one of the cottages was occupied by the summer waitresses at Lawson's—Madison and Brittany, and that they had returned from their ushering jobs. She knew the other one was deserted. The lights were on inside the girls' cottage and she presumed they were on their way to bed. The lights went off just as she saw headlights moving down the lane toward the vacant cottage.

Curious, Marilyn hunkered down to make sure she wasn't caught in the driver's line of vision. The car stopped just next to the garage door as it opened and out walked that big guy. The driver went inside and closed the door. She edged closer to the back of the cottage near the Toyota. From inside the garage she could hear an exchange of what sounded like harsh words. She couldn't make out much, but she heard someone say, "too many deliveries. . . keep calling me. . .not my problem." The big guy, she presumed, mumbled in a way that made him difficult to understand. As the garage door opened, Marilyn pushed herself farther into the bushes to avoid being seen. The driver returned to the car and the trunk opened and the big guy put in a package. He closed the trunk, and the car drove off again in a hurry. Marilyn presumed that the business here involved illegal drugs. 'Otherwise,' she thought, 'why so sneaky?'

The big guy retreated back toward the garage just as a tabby cat strolled around the corner to join him. She watched him lean over and stroke the cat, talking to it at the same time. 'Not the big brute he appears to be, perhaps,' thought Marilyn. 'He seems to have a gentle streak to him. How did someone like that get into this business.'

Marilyn returned to the car and drove home to a soak in her tub, a glass of wine and bed. It had been a long day—punctuated with the opening night of the play, the drama with Bertha and then the strange goings on at the deserted cottage. 'What a complicated knot my simple life has become. . .'

¤ ¤ ¤

The girls hadn't yet come down from the high of having ushered for the opening night of *Clue*. There were actors they recognized from both screen and theatre in the audience—all there to both honor their fellow actors and hoping they would, too, be invited in the future to appear on the stage. The Falmouth Playhouse was a gem of a venue. Appearances were very much in demand when actors were between gigs. The actors were accustomed to the goggle-eyed stares of the summer ushers and treated Madison and Brittany with great tolerance and kindness. It made Madison and Brittany feel special, of course, utterly innocent to the self-flattery of actors behind the treatment. Rhys Traynor had made a special effort to come over to talk with them at the reception and they were surprised at how nice he was. He seemed so natural and easy going. They loved listening to his accent and kept him engaged for as long as they could.

They had a hard time pulling themselves away from the theatre in the hopes they would get to know some of the actors beyond their polite conversation with fans, but they had an early start in the morning and finally dragged themselves home. They were nowhere near tired after the stimulating day and evening, so they got themselves ready for bed, turned out the lights and took their beers outside to the porch to talk themselves down. They still hadn't really shared much about their respective days apart when Brittany went to New York with Sam and Madison spent the day with Josiah. And they wanted to hash over the things that had happened in the theatre after the play.

They were in their chatty rhythm when they heard a car rumbling down the road behind the cottage. They glanced over to see the same Toyota pull up with the driver's door next to the garage. The biggest of the bunch from the boat opened the door and came out of the garage.

"Let's sneak over that way, Maddy. Shall we?"

"Great idea."

They left the porch and went around to the back of the house on the side facing away from the stranger and crept closer along the edge of the road. They got there just in time to glimpse the back of one of them as he went into the garage and closed the door.

"There's something familiar about the guy that just went into the garage." said Brittany. "But I can't figure it out."

They heard muffled talking from inside, but they were too far away to make it out. Then, just as the garage door was opening again, they saw movement in the bushes at the other side of the cottage.

"Look there," whispered Madison.

"Who is THAT?" said Brittany.

"Let's wait and see what's up."

They couldn't see the driver, but they watched the other guy put a package into the trunk. As the car pulled out, Madison whispered again, "Get down. He's turning around."

They hunkered down at the side of the road. The car sped out and the guy went to close the door to the garage. Dixie distracted him, and he leaned over to get closer to her as he closed the garage door.

"Well, that solves the mystery, doesn't it?" said Brittany quietly. "Hey, look. That person in the bushes is moving."

The girls sat in stunned silence as they recognized Marilyn and saw her creep back up the dune. They scrambled to the top of the dune themselves and watched her fade into the woods.

But Marilyn wasn't the only one watching the Toyota that night. Kellerman had seen it all from his perch at the end of the road.

¤ ¤ ¤

The Hy-Fal Tavern had been the watering hole of locals since before prohibition. It was housed in a restored brick warehouse whose interior walls stretched up two stories. They were embedded with iron beams that had been cut off at the wall when they were no longer needed to hoist the heavy bundles that were delivered and stored in the warehouse. The tavern had previously been located in a building that burned to the ground, and rebuilding was too much for the proprietors to take on at the time. They had no regrets about their move. They had additional parking, the building had a certain industrial appeal to both the locals and the tourists, the food was dependably good, so business was brisk. The wait staff were long-standing employees and knew the locals by name. Long before the popularity of specialty beers, the Hy-Fal served British and local brews on tap along with English fare— bangers and mash, fish and chips, Welsh rarebit. Given the resurgence of brew pub appeal, the tavern held more appeal for the tourists than ever before.

Bertha arrived around ten and was ready for bear. Instead she ordered bangers and fries, known as "chips" on the Hy-Fal menu, along with an imperial pint of Guinness stout. She sat at the bar so she could chat with the barkeep.

"How'd the openin' night go, Bertie?" asked the barkeep.

"I'm spittin' mad, Emory. The play went fine. It was downhill after that."

"That Traynor guy still gettin' to you, is he?"

"He's an evil guy. He pretends to act the gentleman and then slices right to the heart if he doesn't get his way. He really sets me off."

"Keep cool, Bertie. Or you'll end up regrettin' it—like the last time. It ain't worth it, ya'know."

"I know, but really. I was just inviting him to join us at the fundraiser for Haiti on Monday when the theatre is dark. And he said such unforgiveable things about Haitians not being deserving. I mean, he's really vile."

"I'm just sayin', Bertie. Maybe he's a scumbag, but he's not worth it for you.

Anyway, here's your bangers. That'll make you feel a little better, eh?" he said sliding the plate in front of her along with the mustard and cutlery.

¤ ¤ ¤

Unlike his usual drop-off point in Hyannis, the driver of the Toyota had a special delivery in Falmouth. He had a bad feeling about it. Falmouth was too small to provide any kind of anonymity. Nonetheless, it had been made perfectly clear that he was expected to fulfill the order. He tried to make the best of it.

Backing up the alley, he stopped the car, blocking entry for anyone else. He walked around to the back and took the package out, closed the trunk and went down the narrow passageway between the buildings to a door in the center. After two taps on the door it opened. He put his free hand out, took the envelope and passed the package to the unseen person.

He went back down the passageway and got into his car—just as he noticed another car pull into the alleyway opposite. He pulled out without turning on his headlights and pulled over to the side of the street between the alleys to park.

¤ ¤ ¤

Christine Webb-Curtis and Dimity Hammon

Annie was unloading the dishes, food, and other paraphernalia from the opening night after party in the alley behind the Fair Falmouth Café. The back of the station wagon was open, and she was moving things in through the back door to the kitchen area. As she pulled the final stack of trays out of the car, she felt someone watching her.

Flustered, she dropped the tray off the top, which bounced off the gravel and shot across the alley.

A man emerged from a car in the shadows and Annie stood stock still.

He picked up the tray, and as he stood up she stammered, "You scared me to death! What are you doing here and why were you in the dark?"

"Sorry about that, Annie. I certainly didn't mean to. I had a little errand to run."

"Here?!"

"Well, not here. But I saw you pull in here alone and was most concerned that you were alone in a dark alley at night. I felt it my duty, really, to help you."

"Oh, I see."

"Here, give me those trays and I'll take them inside for you."

"Thanks, but no thanks. I'll manage on my own. And I have to get back. Joe's expecting me."

"Of course. As you wish." He backed away a little, then turned to walk the length of the alley to his car.

Annie retrieved the tray, hurried back into the café, locked up and drove off, very relieved to be in her locked car on the way home without additional incident.

¤ ¤ ¤

Dolores offered to give Eric and his family a ride to and from Lawson's since Eric had rented out the car. As they pulled up to the cottage, Jennie said, "We appreciate the ride, Miss Darrington."

"My pleasure, dear. It's been fun getting to know you all better. And Sara, you've been delightful."

"Thank you, Miss Darrington," Sara said with her impish smile. She turned back and waved as they walked to the cottage door.

"Thanks so much, Meaghan," said Eric. "You were wonderful to have Parker for the evening. It was great having him stay here so Sara and Jennie could see the play."

Jennie stepped through the doorway behind Eric to get Sara ready for a bath before bed. "Why don't you walk Meaghan back to her car, Eric."

"Oh, no, thanks, Mrs. Shiller. I'll be fine."

"I insist," said Eric. "And I can pay you along the way."

"Oh, you're very nice. But I've been paid. Thanks, though."

They stepped outside along the edge of the fairway and walked toward the parking lot.

"How'd the play go, Mr. Shiller?"

"It went great, Meaghan. Everyone seemed to enjoy it. And Jennie and Sara had a good time, too."

"Thanks for walking me here, Mr. Shiller. I really appreciate it."

"Thanks again for watching Parker. I know he had a much better time with you than he ever would have at the theatre."

"'Nite, then."

"'Nite."

Returning to the cottage, Jennie was just putting Sara to bed. Sara beckoned for a kiss, and then Eric closed the door.

"Would you like some hot cocoa before we go to bed, Eric? Especially after such a thrilling evening."

"I'd love it. Thanks."

They moved out to the deck to enjoy their hot chocolate along with the peace of the golf course and the shining moon.

"Did you enjoy the after party, Jen?"

"It was perfect. Everyone was so happy. And Sara was absolutely in her element. She does love all the attention. And she got a lot of it from pretty much everybody. Well, everybody except Troy Douglas and Mr. Traynor."

"Well, Douglas doesn't care about anybody but himself and Rhys is not likely to come around. And frankly, I don't think he's the kind of person we want Sara exposed to anyway. He isn't the warm and fuzzy type, that's for sure."

"No, I'm sure that . . ." Jennie's voice faded off and she looked down at her lap.

"What is it, Jennie? What's the matter?"

"I shouldn't really say anything, but there was something about Mr. Traynor that made me uncomfortable."

"Well, what happened, then?"

215

"I was standing near the stage during the party watching Sara make her rounds. She was having such a good time, ya know?"

"Yes. But what about Traynor?"

"Yes, well, I happened to look over toward the door and noticed him talking with Bertha Poppe. And they were having what looked like very angry words. She was poking him in the chest. And he swiped her hand away—almost hit her. And then she slammed out the door. And right away, he noticed that I had been watching, and he started toward me fast. And he looked pretty angry. I was scared. But Mr. Putnam stepped in front of me right then to talk. Then Mr. Traynor announced that he was leaving."

Eric's jaw tightened and he said, "Why didn't you tell me then?"

"Eric! You were enjoying yourself. I'm sure it was nothing."

"That's not nothing. He was obviously threatening you."

"No, no. I don't think so. . . Well, maybe he was. Anyway, it's all over now. I'm sure it isn't important."

"Let's hope."

"Maybe you should stay away from the theatre for a few days."

"Yeah. Maybe. But Sara will be heartbroken."

"I saw a pamphlet for the Children's Museum in the lobby. How about taking them there on Tuesday? Tomorrow's the matinee anyway, and you'd probably want to have them here for naps. And then Monday, we're dark. So Tuesday would be perfect."

"OK. I'll do that. That's a good idea. I'll look for the brochure tomorrow, then. And we'll make an adventure of it."

"And don't worry about Traynor. Trust me. I'm sure he won't bother you anymore."

"You are way overprotective!"

He leaned over and kissed her on the forehead and took her hand in his. "All will be fine, Jen. Wow. Look at the moon. What a sight."

"Mmmm. It's full of peace, the evening. We're in paradise, aren't we?"

"Yes, Jen. We are."

Christine Webb-Curtis and Dimity Hammon

Chapter 19 – The Curtain Comes Down

The mahogany front door sported a transom window of clear beveled glass and a bronze pineapple door knocker. The door was lined on either side with clear beveled sidelight windows. Just as Madison reached up to the knocker, Lil opened the door in a flourish and greeted the girls enthusiastically.

"Come on in, girls. We're glad you're here."

"Thanks, Ms. . . . Lil," said Brittany.

"That's right. 'Lil.'"

The girls stepped though the first foyer with benches on both sides and storage below into Nico and Lil's interior foyer. This was their first visit to Nico's home. They gaped at the shiny honey-colored pine staircase rising gracefully upstairs to a balcony corridor leading around to the bedrooms, bathroom and library. On the first floor on one side of the staircase was a spacious living room that ran the depth of the house and on the other side a dining room that led toward the kitchen.

"Wow. This is wonderful. What a beautiful place," said Madison.

"We are lucky, aren't we?" replied Lil. "We're here, you know, because the Chief Detective who left and whose job Nico stepped into stayed in Italy with his wife and daughter and decided not to come back."

Wide eyed, Madison said, "That's something. He's not coming back? Wow."

"Yes. Well, I understand it. He wanted to be with his family—especially if there are any grandchildren. And speaking of grandchildren, come on in to the kitchen so I can introduce you to our family."

Lil led them through the dining room and a butler's pantry where they were startled by a small child suddenly emerging from a door in the wall, jumping down and running back through the kitchen. The door covered a dumbwaiter that led upstairs to the second floor library where tea was served in the afternoon for the nineteenth- and early twentieth-century residents of the house. The dumbwaiter was the plaything of every child that ever lived in that house as a means to be transported by a sibling from one floor to the other. The Forgione grandchildren were no exception.

"Nino!" Lil admonished. "Be careful and slow down." Her voice faded in the memory of her grandson as he all but vanished into the back stairwell to race noisily back up in the hopes that he could do it again.

Rehearsals for Retribution

The girls followed Lil through the doorway of the butler's pantry into the large kitchen full of bustling adults and more children of all sizes. Nico was at the center island taking advantage of a generous piece of prosciutto with a long, thin knife, which he then arranged around pieces of fragrant melon and placed on a wooden serving platter. He looked up at the girls and beckoned them over for a sample. On their way to the cutting board, they were greeted effusively by all, and Lil offered them something to drink.

"Iced tea for me, thanks," said Brittany.

"That'd be great for me, too," added Madison.

"Since we're all family here," said Lil handing the girls their drinks, "the first drink is on me. Then you're on your own. The refrigerator is yours to rummage through for any more."

"Thanks, Lil," said Brittany. "It's great to be here with your family. It makes me miss mine for sure. The summer's a long time."

"Of course." Lil caught sight of the necklace around Brittany's neck. "That's an interesting necklace. Is it a locket?"

"My cat, Dixie, found it next door. Since it's sort of deserted over there, I don't think there's anyone around to return it to, so I adopted it."

"And why not? If there's no owner. Is there a picture inside?" Lil asked as she pressed on it to open it. "Ooh. What's this?" she asked in surprise.

"Isn't that odd?" said Brittany. "It looks sort of like a little spoon. But no picture, which is exactly what I wondered."

Lil frowned as she asked, "Could you take it off, Brittany? I'd like to show it to Nico."

"Sure. No problem." She reached back to unhook the clasp and put it in Lil's hand.

Lil walked it over to Nico.

"Caro. Look at what Brittany found next door to her cottage," she said holding the open locket in her hand. "Isn't this used for snorting cocaine?"

"What?" exclaimed Madison. "Cocaine? You must be kidding."

"Don't worry, Madison," said Nico. "It's just a necklace. But even so, do you think I could hold onto it for a bit?"

"Do you think it means something? You think there's stuff going on over there that we should be investigating?"

"We can do that, ya know," said Brittany.

"How about you just keep your eyes open and leave it at that. I wouldn't want you to get involved in something that could get you into trouble. Anyway, it's probably nothing."

"OK. We'll try. But when you're finished, d'you think I could have that back? I kinda like it. It was a present from Dixie after all."

"Sure. I'll make sure to keep it safe for you. So would you like to help me with dinner?" Nico asked, offering them a knife and a yellow pepper in one hand and an onion in the other.

Brittany took the pepper and the knife. "Sure. I'm glad to. How do you want it?"

"Sliced, please, like this. For sautéing."

"Yes, sir, then," said Brittany playfully.

Madison took the onion and reached for another knife and moved to the other side of Brittany and began peeling and slicing the onion thinking she could have stayed home to do this. . .

¤ ¤ ¤

After a cozy evening with Nico and Lil and their family, the girls arrived home to find Dixie in their bedroom smelling like skunk.

"Oooh. What the heck is that awful smell?" said Madison.

As she approached the bedroom and saw Dixie splayed out on the bed, she knew the answer.

"Unfortunately, it's Dixie. She seems to have been romping with a skunk. Shit! I have no idea what to do about that," she said shrugging her shoulders and looking at Madison for help. "Do you?"

"We could call Josiah or Sam. Maybe they'd know."

"Good idea," said Madison.

Sam had the formula for skunk clean-up, but when Dixie got away from them and headed back outside for the night, Brittany just put it off until the next day and hung her duvet out on the line to get rid of the smell.

"Back to work tomorrow," said Brittany, "and maybe she'll be less stinky then."

"Anyway, she's gone for tonight. I really wanted to finish my book, but I'm gonna sit on the porch and have a beer. Wanna join me?"

"I think I'd better 'cause I can't stay in the bedroom until it's aired out. I hope it goes away by the time the guys come over tomorrow."

□ □ □

"Glad you're here, Ted," said Nico as they walked through to the kitchen where Lil and Meche were chatting. Nico and Lil figured that Ted needed some company seeing as how the theatre was dark on Mondays and they had invited Meche to join them at the last minute.

"Look what I found at the front door, Lil. I thought I'd invite him in for dinner. Whadya think, Cara?"

Approaching him, Lil squeezed his shoulder to welcome him. "Ted. We're so glad to have you here. It's gotta be so lonely with Susan gone for so long. And how is her mother anyway?"

"She's hanging in there, but now we're just waiting."

"Well, we thought you might need some good home cooking and family time."

Lil knew how to lift the mood and she did a good job at it.

"So," Lil said looking at what was in Ted's hand. "Is that a funny-looking bouquet of flowers or what?"

"Oh this," Ted said holding up the bag that Casey had brought home. "This is something Casey dragged back to the house along with an overpowering skunk stench. And since I don't know what it is and was concerned it might be something he shouldn't be playing with, I thought I'd bring it along for your esteemed detective husband to check out." And from behind his back, his other hand came around. "And these, Lil, are for you, of course."

"Oh, Ted. They're lovely. I'll get them in water and we can all enjoy them. How very thoughtful."

Putting the bag on the counter, he said to Nico, "I don't know what this is, Nico, but I have an uncomfortable feeling it might be something illegal. So I leave it to you."

Glancing at it nonchalantly—or so it seemed, Nico said, "I'll take a look at it. Where's it from, by the way."

"I'm sure you will have no trouble imagining that my four-legged companion brought it home to me. Who knows where he got it."

"Well, I'll have a look-see later. Thanks, Ted—I think. . .

"Now would you like an aperitif? We're all enjoying an Aperol. Of if you prefer, a

Compari? And Meche, you know Ted, of course."

"Nice to see you, Ted, outside of the theatre."

"Same here," he said reaching out his hand. Turning to Nico, "I'd like the same as you, thanks. That'd be great."

¤ ¤ ¤

Stepping out of the kitchen, Nico called Kellerman.

"Could you come by and pick something up? Ted Dickenson's dog brought home what appears to be a bag of cocaine. Found it in some evening scamper. I'd like to know if we can have it traced."

"Sure thing."

"If we can trace it, how soon can we have the results?"

"I'll have something to report in the morning. I'll come over and get your little package and take it in to forensics to get them started. I do think there's something going on at that cottage down on Onion Bay."

"How d'you mean?"

"Last night, I went down there. Looks like the girls were right about the cottage next door. If this bag is cocaine and the dog found it down there, it'd be one more piece of the puzzle."

Kellerman decided to drive it to Boston that night instead of having it couriered, and he called his partner, Marc, to ask if he wanted to go along for the ride.

"We can drop it off and make a night of it. And I can pick up the results in the morning."

"Sounds good," said Marc. "Pick me up. I'll be ready."

¤ ¤ ¤

"Hey guys. Finally," said Madison. "I hope you brought the beer 'cause we've got the dinner--but no beer."

Dangling from each of Sam's hands was a six-pack of beer. He and Josiah stepped up on the porch steps and inside the cottage through the door held open by Madison.

"I'm starving. What's on the menu?" asked Josiah, leaning over to embrace Madison.

Brittany motioned them to come into the kitchen area where she gave each of them a plate and said, "Golden Swan's on the menu. The best Indian food this side of Bourne. Or that's what we've heard. Help yourselves. We're planning to eat out on the porch—especially since Dixie's skunk run-in. It's still a little smelly in here. Dontcha notice it?"

"Not really," said Sam. "Did you use the stuff I told you to?"

"She got away from us before we could. So we haven't yet."

Josiah shook his head and said, "I don't notice anything—fortunately."

Out on the porch they sat with their dinner and beer until, full and contented, they snuggled--Josiah with Madison and Sam with Brittany.

¤ ¤ ¤

Making his way to the cottage, the driver of the Toyota cursed his predicament.

'This is it. Not doing this again,' he thought as he turned off the main road. 'I'm done with it!'

As he pulled up to the garage of the deserted cottage to pick up the goods, he was sure he saw a movement on the porch next door. He looked a little more closely and recognized someone.

'The waitresses,' he thought. 'This cannot be good. They've probably been there all along.'

Gripping the wheel, his thoughts continued. 'Bloody hell.'

¤ ¤ ¤

From behind the cottage, they heard a car rolling up the lane. Madison and Josiah who were cuddling in the hammock on the corner of the porch, leaned around to see the Toyota tooling up the lane as if he owned it.

"He's baaaack," she said to anyone who was listening.

Brittany leaned around the corner to see the car pull up in front of the garage.

"Well, so he is!" she said.

The man slunk into the garage as soon as it opened. He glanced over as if he noticed some movement on the porch next door and then hurried in through the garage door.

Brittany pushed back quickly. "I think he saw me. Shit. Maybe we should go inside for a while and close up the house."

"Sure. Let's. But what about that awful smell?"

"And what do you suggest, then? And when did you turn into such a little princess?"

"Let's all take a walk down the beach," suggested Sam. "And hoodies might be a good idea."

"OK. Let's," said Madison. "I'll get ours, Brit."

They closed the house and left the porch heading away from their neighbor's cottage. Rounding the point at the end, they looked back to see the old car's headlights moving slowly past the cottage and then picking up speed, disappearing into the thick wooded area toward the road. They also noticed that the boat was back again.

"Crap," said Brittany. "That big guy could also be around there. Except for Dixie, I'd kinda like to go somewhere else right now. This is getting a bit creepy."

"Y'know," said Josiah. "You could stay with us tonight. Tomorrow when it's daytime, we can come back and scope things out and make sure everything's OK."

"Oh, Jos," oozed Madison. "That'd be great. I'd feel sooo much better. I didn't know this would freak me out quite so much."

Returning to the house, they found Dixie sitting on the porch looking ever so cute and cuddly. Running up the stairs, Brittany gathered her up and almost cuddled her but for the lingering stench of skunk.

"Dixie, Dixie, Dixie. How'd you get out?"

From across the divide between the cottages, they heard, "Kitty. Kitty. C'mere."

They all froze where they were, looking at each other and then at Dixie.

"Let's go, girls," said Josiah. "Bring her with you for cryin' out loud. We'll come back in the morning for your stuff. Come on."

The girls grabbed their purses and pulled the door behind them. They all piled into Josiah's car and peeled out, Dixie squirming to beat the band.

¤ ¤ ¤

Kellerman returned with the results by noon on Tuesday and reported to Nico.

"The stuff's from Columbia," he said tossing the paper on Nico's desk. "All very interesting, eh?"

"Very."

"Curiously enough, BPD's been tracking this particular cocaine. It arrives—believe it or not—in lobster tails."

"Come again?"

"Yeah. Really. They're on the verge of figuring out how it all works. So I'd say this is obviously tied in to that whole thing. Chief Walsh suspects a connection back to some rogue cop."

Kellerman locked a look with Nico, lifting one eyebrow knowingly. "This might be just the payback you've been waiting for."

"Wouldn't surprise me," said Nico getting up from behind his desk. "I certainly would appreciate knowing that the cops who accused me of being a traitor last year were caught. It'd be sweet justice."

"If we're gonna do anything about it, we need to act fast. "I've run a trace on that Toyota, Nico. There's no doubt that it's mixed up in this mess.

"I think we have to pick up the driver. So let's ramp this up. Whaddya think, Lieutenant?"

"Absolutely and I know where we can be sure to find him!"

¤ ¤ ¤

In the parking lot, Dolores watched the recording one more time before entering the theatre in preparation for the performance.

¤ ¤ ¤

Just offstage, Kellerman waited until Nico moved his way, whispering to him as discreetly as he could. Nico's eyes moved quickly to Kellerman's hand as he pulled the handcuffs smoothly out of his pocket and left them dangling unobtrusively by his side.

The final curtain came down and Kellerman walked quickly toward Eric who was gathering himself for a bow. As the curtain came up, he fully absorbed the meaning of Kellerman's approach and stared at him in shock. At the same time Rhys moved jerkily toward the front of the stage in an effort to get out just as Kellerman declared, "You're under arrest," in a loud voice.

The fleeing actor stopped in mid-stride, turned to face Kellerman and said, "How dare you imply that I am a criminal."

Marilyn moved back onto the stage from the other side to help Rhys. Troy, determined to be the one to protect his object of desire, at least until he heard any explanation, grabbed her arm. Confused Kellerman reached out to put the cuff on Eric's wrist. Dolores double-timed it toward them, tripped, falling toward Rhys, and grabbing his arm, helped herself up. She turned toward the audience. She pulled out the video camera, and the audience listened as the sound came through. There was no denying whose voice it was.

"Dollie, you are just delicious! Perhaps we should shock all of Hollywood, run off to Las Vegas and get married? Wha'd'ya say?"

"Interesting proposition, Rhys, but haven't you gone through a couple of wives already?"

"Oh they were a completely different story."

"Really, do tell?"

"I was very young when I married Gwen. I admit she was quite lovely and pleasing in the beginning, but as I became more famous, she became more attached, well clingy really, and that just wasn't working for me. I was very popular with the young starlets I worked with··rightly so··and she didn't appreciate that I had to keep them happy, if you know what I mean?"

"I can't imagine why she couldn't understand how important that was to your career, Rhys! She must've been very naive." said Dolores.

"Right you are, old girl! Exactly the problem. She was very naive and it made her very anxious. She started taking anti-anxiety medication. She'd never been much of a drinker. You know, that's a requirement in the entertainment industry. I felt she needed to learn how to keep up at parties and events. Of course, with the anti-anxiety pills, she sometimes got a bit, ah, fuzzy. She was so very resentful of time I spent with other women. Sometimes, just to be kind, I invited her to join us in a ménage à trois. But she

235

was quite upset at the idea. She even raised her voice in protest, which I found very off putting, so to speak."

"How foolish of her," she demurred. "It must have been most difficult for you."

"I tried and tried to make her see that she was standing in the way of the career that I was meant to have. Of course you'd understand that, my dear."

"Yes, of course," So what _did_ you do?"

"Well, she was using those tranquilizers, you know, and one night she took more than she knew. I had helped her forget with some Rohypnol, just to make sure. It's a very handy drug, you know. Makes people forget what they're doing, or what they did, as was the case with that lovely redhead. Also releases inhibitions. But that's another story, isn't it? Anyway when Gwen combined it with the martinis that we'd had, she lost consciousness and I wasn't able to bring her around in time. All right, I admit that her martinis were quite a bit stronger than mine. By the time I was able to call the medics an hour or so later, she was gone. The coroner ruled it an overdose--very common in the business, you know. Elvis Presley and now poor Whitney. Anyway I was able to get over my grief with some help from accommodating young ladies."

"What about her family? What'd they do? They must have been beside themselves!"

"Oh yes, they were very upset. They knew her as the sweet young thing I'd married and couldn't understand how she could have changed that much. But of course they were real yokels, so how could they?"

"What about your second wife?"

"Ah yes, so strange. One day, she said she was going over to Crane's Beach for the afternoon. It was just a short spin in the little speedboat to get there from the cottage in Ipswich. But she never came back! Just disappeared off the face of the earth! The police looked for the boat but could never find it. I could have told them where to look, but by then they'd called off the search. My people had the boat repainted and sold it on Craigslist. Of course her body was not going to ever turn up. . .

"I suppose you'd be nervous about becoming my wife after hearing that story, but I promise nothing would ever happen to you, my dear. I am mad about you, obsessed, really! Put me out of my misery and say you'll take care of me for the rest of my life. Please," he slurred.

Dolores turned off the recording and handed it over to Nico before he asked for it.

"That's not the half of it," she said solemnly. "I recorded his every move almost from the moment he arrived, that bastard." He was running drugs when he wasn't trying to seduce women. Eric is innocent. They were just using his car. I'll show you the proof."

Shocked, Marilyn stepped back. "How could this be? He was so kind to me when I was so distressed, I was so deceived."

"You certainly were deceived, my friend. He wasn't kind to you. He drugged you and then raped you!" He's been doing it for years to women all over the globe. You are lucky he didn't kill you, but I'm glad to say you weren't important enough to him for that," announced Dolores. "I'll give you the proof later, you'll see what really happened."

Troy stepped into the spotlight and declared, "See, he just needed to acknowledge his true identity, his real proclivities, and none of this would have happened," he cried.

"Oh, for god's sake," snarled Rhys. "I have no interest in you or any of your kind!"

"Don't be so sure of that," replied Dolores. "You might not have a choice."

"And don't forget Haiti," chimed in Bertha. "You'll pay for your attitude!"

Rhys turned to her, astonished. "What the hell are you going on about!" he howled.

Kellerman began, "You have the right to remain. . ."

"Never mind. She drugged me!!" said Rhys. "I'll be out of here by tonight. Don't think you can keep me!"

"We'll see," said Nico. "You can come with us and tell us about your escapades in the Toyota. If you come clean and tell us about your sources, we might be able to shave a year or so off your sentence. Your call, of course."

"Get me my lawyer." Rhys was incensed. Enough was enough. " Do you know who my lawyer is?"

"I'm sure he's very nice," said Nico calmly. "And we all would be delighted to meet him, but in the meantime, if you wouldn't mind coming with us, we have several things to discuss, my friend."

Kellerman added, "Ms. Darrington, we'll need you to come with us too, I'm afraid. After all, you did coerce a confession. Somehow I think that'll be overlooked considering the situation."

Christine Webb-Curtis and Dimity Hammon

Chapter 20 - Annie's Story

On the way home Joe turned to Annie and said, "I'm so sorry, sweetheart. I know you loved him. Who would have thought?"

"I would've," said Annie quietly.

"Huh? What do you mean?"

"Joe, why don't we wait 'til we get home. It's a long story and I want to tell you; but let's go home, get a glass of wine and sit in the breezeway. I need some time to get it all out."

"Sure, you settle in. I'll check on Sophie and then I'll listen. It sure has been an interesting day!"

An hour later they were sitting comfortably in their chaise longues with a couple of glasses of merlot and the evening breeze.

Annie began. "I have kept this secret so long, Joe. It's hard for me to tell anyone."

"You know you can tell me anything," Joe replied. "I'll always love you."

"My Uncle Rhys was like a god to me. He would shower us with presents from the countries where he'd been shooting films. I was really popular because I had a movie star in my family. I'm ashamed to say I took advantage of that.

"On one visit he took our family out to dinner at Lawson's. He kept ordering wine and my parents, who weren't used to drinking, got quite, well, smashed."

"Understandable," said Joe as he topped up their glasses.

"Or intentional," replied Annie.

"Anyway, they went right up to bed, passed out, really, and Uncle Rhys and I settled down on the loveseat to watch one of his movies. In a little while, he seemed to drift off and slumped in my direction. I thought it was funny until he sort of snored and his arm landed across my waist with his hand near my breast. Then he moved his hand and touched my breast and then squeezed it. I didn't know what to do, I couldn't move without waking him up so I just stayed there, stiff as a board. He leaned further until he was almost on top of me and then, suddenly he was all over me! I tried to shout, to scream, but he covered my mouth. He said if I said anything he would tell my parents that I, that I came onto him! Then he made me, you know. . . I thought I was going to die."

"That scum," said Joe through gritted teeth. "He'll pay!"

"Don't you think he's going to pay now, Joe?"

"Yes, but it won't be enough. It'll never be enough. You poor thing!"

"Oh no, Joe. Don't pity me. I got past it and I'm proud of it."

"Yes, you're right. You're strong and beautiful to boot! Let's talk about this later and figure out whether you want to do anything about it. In the meantime we know he's probably going to spend the rest of his life in prison. Let's go to bed. It's been a very long day."

Christine Webb-Curtis and Dimity Hammon

Chapter 21 -- Marilyn Learns the Truth

The next day, after Dolores gave her story to the police along with the evidence, she called Marilyn.

"Hi there. So, are you ready to hear the real story."

"Well, I guess so, but I'm a bit nervous. Is it really bad?"

"It's not nice, but at least you'll understand what really happened to you."

"Why don't you come over to my house? You know where I live, don't you? That way we can have some privacy."

"OK, I'll be there in a bit."

They settled on the deck with a glass of chilled white wine and Dolores turned on the video camera playback. Marilyn watched and listened to the replay, amazed at what was playing out before her eyes. It was like a bad X-rated movie and she was the star.

She saw herself awake to find herself naked in the bed; and Rhys, looking freshly showered, was fastening his cufflinks.

"Ah," he said with a smirk. "Your husband should not have been so hasty with his wandering eye. You are delightful and inventive!"

Grabbing the sheet to cover herself, she cried, "What the hell happened?"

"Just about everything, my dear," oozed Rhys, grinning. "As I said you are quite inventive!"

Marilyn tried to get up, but fell back, her head swimming.

"What, my dear? Ready for another go round so soon? Too much for me! Anyway you'll have to run along. I have a new script to go over and lines to rehearse."

"You drugged me!" spat Marilyn.

"I normally don't have to resort to that, but in the interest of expediency, it seemed appropriate at the time. Also I find it helps eliminate some unnecessary inhibitions. Not that you needed that, m'dear."

"How dare you? You won't get away with this. I'm reporting you to the police for rape!"

"In my experience, dear, the police don't usually believe that I would have to violate anyone. And besides that, if you truly want to rid yourself of that louse of a husband and get as much as you can out of the deal, you'd best not be telling people that you slept with someone else on the very day you found out about his escapades. Not that anyone would blame you, but it wouldn't help your case. Now really, dear. Up and away with you. I have obligations."

"You are a despicable creature."

"Do come and see the play. And I hope you'll bring along those charming friends of yours. They were so supportive of you while you were pouring out your tale of woe."

"You slimy, sneaky scumbag. You knew what happened and took advantage of me!"

"Yes dear, now can I help you on with those shoes so you can find your way home?"

Marilyn couldn't believe what she was seeing. "Sunovabitch," she hissed. "And to think I thought he liked me, that he cared! One thing for sure, if they need any more evidence I'll be happy to testify as a character witness and hope he gets everything he deserves in prison!"

Christine Webb-Curtis and Dimity Hammon

Epilogue

The girls were glad it was over, but still felt too creeped out to stay out at Onion Bay. They moved in with Josiah and Sam for the remainder of the summer, leaving only the most meager of belongings in the cottage in case their parents showed up unexpectedly.

The thugs were easily tracked down and would be in jail for a nice long stay. While there, Enzo took a veterinary technician course and enrolled in the stray cat adoption program, fostering cats until they found new homes. He would be out on good behavior well before the rest of his co-criminals.

Eric couldn't believe he had been caught up in some suspicious scheme on the Cape once again. Thankfully, having been exonerated, he was able to enjoy the rest of the summer and even gained a bit of fame for his innocent participation.

Bertha wrote an "I told you so" article for the Cape Cod Gazette. She was interviewed by the Boston Globe about her part in the investigation and used the opportunity to make a plea for aid to Haitians.

Troy crawled back to California to seek help from his therapist to deal with his loss. The publicity about the play and its outcome garnered him new and better roles in film.

Joe moved on to the next play, asking Eric to take the lead role. He also suggested Eric take a look at the script for the film he was producing in the fall.

Nico passed Dolores' recording on to Captain Walsh of the Boston Police Department. While it was not admissible in court, it established some level of guilt and gave the police enough to justify reopening the case of Gwen's death. Dolores was finally and happily reunited with her brother's family.

Kellerman was offered a detective position in the Naples, Florida, Police Department. He and his partner, Marc, left for Florida at the end of July with a promise to Nico and Lil of the use of their guest room when the Cape Cod winter got too much for them.

Francis McCormick and his Boston Police Department cronies finally found their way to prison after a high-profile and quick trial.

Jim Horneby disappeared from the Cape. Grateful that he had miraculously not been caught, he escaped to Louisiana with a delicate and all-too-naïve Vietnamese woman.

Rhys was charged with two counts of first-degree murder and drug trafficking and ended up in prison. His acting career was certainly over. While in prison, he continued to promote himself by teaching acting and producing plays for his new found friends to enjoy.

As usual, Sal managed to remain in the background and unscathed. He was more determined than ever to bring his nephew into the fold.

Marilyn enjoyed an uncontested divorce from Jim and ended up with everything. The detailed evidence she had gathered during the crime had been crucial to Rhys' conviction. Thinking about how he would be treated in prison gave her a smug sense of satisfaction. With Jim gone she had time to throw herself into her other hobbies--most of all, tennis. She was looking forward to the winter finals in Florida. Best of all her good friends and teammates would be there with her. She would find herself in the position of amateur detective in the future.

Regrettably, an annual drama involving drugs and murder seemed to be emerging as de rigueur on the Cape. Even so, Nico was satisfied with the resolution of the summer's crime caper. He settled down to enjoy the rest of the season, hoping it would roll out with less drama and fewer drug busts. In celebration of Nico's sleuthing triumph, Lawson's Inn offered Nico and Lil a greatly-reduced golf package for the summer, including lessons, greens fees, clubs, and a cart. To his surprise, the normally-sedentary detective actually enjoyed the game and took on another small role in two more plays that summer. Lil was happy with his newfound passion and they started planning a winter golfing vacation to Florida.

Rehearsals for Retribution

Rehearsals for Retribution

Christine Webb-Curtis and Dimity Hammon

About the Authors

Dimity Hammon and Christine Webb-Curtis have been friends since they were twelve years old. Despite circumstances and distance, they managed to nurture their friendship and are fulfilling a dream of writing together with their second book, *Rehearsals for Retribution: A Cape Cod Crime Mystery*. They spent the summer after high school graduation working as chambermaids at a golf resort on Cape Cod.

Dimity Hammon was born and raised in the Boston area. She has a graduate degree in Archaeology but has spent the majority of her working life administering nonprofit associations. She and her husband have two children and two grandbabies, and live with a new and an old dog and two cats, Trixie and Dixie. She now lives in the Pacific Northwest.

Christine Webb-Curtis grew up in New England and upstate New York. After a Peace Corps stint in South America, she relocated to San Francisco where she graduated from Mills College and received a Masters Degree from the University of Southern California. She has three grown sons and one granddaughter. Her professional career was spent in nonprofit and public service for the state of California. She and her husband make their home in California's central valley with their Bichon Frise, Milo, and two cats.

Made in the USA
Middletown, DE
25 June 2019